# Never Judge a Book

Stacey Broadbent

ISBN:    978-0-473-39988-7 (Paperback)

# Never Judge a Book

Stacey Broadbent

# Chapter One

Jess

"He's a jerk."

"Yeah, he doesn't deserve you. You can do so much better than him."

I raise my bloodshot eyes to look at my friend. "Yeah, knocked up with someone else's baby. I'm every guy's wet dream." My voice catches in my throat. "I'm sorry," I whisper.

"You've got nothing to apologise for," Sarah soothes, rubbing her hand up and down my arm.

"And so what if you're pregnant? You're beautiful, funny, intelligent and strong."

I almost laugh. "I'm not strong."

"Are you kidding? You're one of the strongest people I know! After everything he put you through? I would be a basket case. But you? You've picked yourself up time and time again and kept on living. You can do this." She gives my shoulders a squeeze. "And we'll help you however we can. Won't we, Kelly?"

"Of course! We are one hundred percent behind you."

I smile through my tears. "Thanks guys. I don't think I could do this without you."

"Yes you could. You're stronger than you think."

Pregnant with my first baby, to a man-child who only thinks of himself. For some stupid reason, I thought that our having a child together would make things better. I actually believed him when he said that he wanted to marry me and start a family. They say love will do that to you, though. Make you blind to things. Make you *want* to believe things that deep down you know aren't real.

I should've listened to my parents. Right from their first meeting with him, they disliked him. And why wouldn't they? He was an hour late. An hour! With no excuse, either, I might add. Way to show respect, man.

My parents were also the ones to pick up the pieces each time he betrayed me. They'd warned me that he was no good, but he was like a drug to me, an addiction. I kept going back, even when I knew what I was setting myself up for, was more heartache.

Two and a half years of breaking up and getting back together. Two and a half years! It's no wonder they were sick of hearing about it.

In that time I got pretty good at knowing when he was going behind my back. I developed a sense for it. I knew where to search if I suspected anything. He wasn't the most creative in hiding things. Maybe he wanted to be caught out. Who knows?

Stealing, lying, cheating. That's a lot for any self-respecting twenty-year-old to put up with. That's just the thing though. I didn't have the respect for myself that I should have had. Add to that my zero confidence, and you've got a winning combination right there. Of course I was going to latch on to the first guy who made me feel like I was beautiful. I was a sucker for those cheesy lines back then. Oh to be seventeen and naïve again.

Then somewhere along the way, I stopped feeling beautiful and started feeling like I was worthless. Like I wasn't enough. I guess it was probably when he cheated on me the first time and my whole world as I knew it had crashed in on me.

He was my first love. It was meant to be exciting and romantic, and I was supposed to have fond memories. I actually believed he would be my forever, you know? What a joke.

I had plans. It wasn't meant to be that way. He wasn't meant to cheat on me with his ex-girlfriend. I certainly wasn't meant to meet her and discover how similar we were. I definitely wasn't meant to *like* her, and I'm sure I wasn't meant to be the one to tell her that he had lied about them being back together, and had actually been sleeping with me the whole time. I sure as hell wasn't meant to be the one to break her heart again.

I know that it was his fault. That he was the one lying to us both. I do. But I also know that I had heard rumours and chose not to believe them. I had continued to sleep with him, in the hopes that he would choose me. In doing so, I lost what little self-respect I had mustered.

I couldn't let go. I needed to have answers. I needed to know why he had done that to us. I had been brought up to treat people the way *you* wanted to be treated, not to do whatever you want and to hell with anyone who got in your way. He apologised and told me everything I wanted to hear. I lapped it up, desperately clinging to the hope that he would love me like I loved him.

It was a vicious circle that I didn't have the strength or the will to climb out of. I kept going back. It didn't matter how much he would hurt me, we would argue and break up, and then he would crawl back and I would forgive him. This was what we did.

This time had seemed different. Or maybe I had just wanted it so badly, that I allowed myself to believe that. I don't even know anymore.

I had almost broken free of him. He had left me alone for a month or so, and I had moved on. I had made plans for my future, and had found a nice place to live. Then he had come back, grovelling, like he always did. I still don't understand why I let him back in, when I could see that life could be good without him. I guess I was scared. I hadn't been with anyone else, and the thought of being in another relationship and being vulnerable, scared the shit out of me. So, I did it. I took him back. Again. Better the devil you know, and all that.

He asked me to marry him, and I accepted. We had no money, so there were no rings, just a promise of a life together. I foolishly allowed him to talk me into trying for a baby, as if that would solve all our problems. I kept thinking that a baby would make him grow up. I had convinced myself that it was a good idea. We got pregnant straight away.

And for a while, things *had* been good. Or so I thought.

A few weeks ago, I had been making the bed, when I found a letter stashed between the mattress and the wall. It was addressed to another girl, her name scrawled artistically across the top of the page in *his* handwriting. The first line read "So you want to know why I'm single?"

I felt sick to my stomach. My hands began to shake and tears clouded my vision so I couldn't make out the rest of what was written. I couldn't understand why he would do this again. I mean, we were having a baby together for fuck's sake!

I gave up on the bed, and sat at the kitchen table for several hours, staring at the words, but not really seeing them. I stayed that way until he came home from work. He didn't even try to deny it. I mean, there wasn't really any point, the evidence was right there on the table between us.

He begged me to stay, and to work it out. He promised it wouldn't happen again. Promises I knew he couldn't keep.

The baby growing inside of me was the reason I finally had the strength to get up and walk away. I suddenly realised that I didn't want my baby boy thinking that it was okay to treat women that way. I had to be strong. For my son.

I packed my things and with tears streaming down my face, I drove to my parents' place. I explained everything to them, and you know what? Even with their hatred for him, they still suggested that we try to work things out, for the baby's sake.

After careful consideration, I agreed to give him another chance, on the proviso that we started counselling.

Today was meant to be our first appointment and I drove out to pick him up. He was in the shower when I got there, so I sat at the table to wait. My eyes landed on the phone bill in the centre of the table. A $700 phone bill, no less. I dragged it closer. There were pages and pages of 0900 numbers. My heart began to pound. I was carrying his baby, and he had been calling sex hotlines for the past month? When he had come sauntering out of the bathroom, I had thrown the bill in his face. I couldn't even speak, I was so angry.

I jumped into the car and with my heart almost beating out of my chest, I drove straight to my girlfriends' house. I couldn't face my parents with this shit again.

Which brings me back to the here and now. My two best friends in the whole world, doing what they always do – building me back up after he's torn me down.

They had taken one look at my tear-stained face and ushered me inside, the jug already boiling for the hot chocolates, and a pack of Tim Tams at the ready.

Sarah and Kelly have been my best friends since preschool, and no matter what life throws at me, I know they've always got my back, and I theirs.

Sitting between them now, with the biscuits balancing precariously on my swollen bump, no one speaks. Their fingers entwined with mine is all the comfort I need.

I watch the Tim Tams wobble as my belly jumps to life with the kicks of the baby inside of me. *My baby.*

Their kind words finally settle in my brain. I *am* strong enough to do this. And I certainly don't need *him* in my life anymore.

# Chapter Two

It's been a week since the day I walked out for good.

My due date is creeping closer and I've been busy setting up a space for us at Mum and Dad's. The bassinette is all made up, cloth nappies are folded in piles, and rows upon rows of tiny singlets and onesies line the shelves. I even have a pile of soft toys and rattles ready and waiting, along with my hospital bag. I have packed and re-packed it so many times now; I'm so paranoid that I'm going to forget something.

I haven't spoken to *him* since I left. His fear of what my dad will probably do to him is most-likely a factor here, but even so, it's his child too. You'd think he'd want to be a part of it. I don't even know if he'll be at the birth, and I'm not really sure if I want him there to be honest. I'm worried that I'll be such an emotional wreck that I'll end up taking him back. I *can't* go through that again. No. My son deserves better than that.

To take my mind off him, I've immersed myself in books. I'd actually forgotten how much I loved to read. It had always been a favourite pastime of mine as a child until life got in the way. There's nothing quite like losing yourself in a story. It's the perfect way to escape when you can't go anywhere.

I've taken to walking the short distance to the public library every few days to peruse the shelves and grab more books to keep me occupied. I know there probably won't be much time for it once baby arrives, so I'm taking full advantage of the peace and quiet while I still can.

I stayed up rather late last night to finish the latest novel in the series I've been reading, so I could be ready for another trek this morning.

I slip my feet into some ballet flats – I've given up trying to tie laces now, it's too difficult to bend around the bump – and don my coat and scarf, before draping my bag across my shoulder. The air outside is cool and every breath I take is visible. I pull my scarf tighter around my neck to keep the chill out. One hand rests on my belly, while the other reaches around to rest on my lower back as I waddle down the street. The closer I get to my due date, the more my back starts to protest. They say it's good to keep active throughout your pregnancy, but I'm not sure how many more walks I'm going to be able to make.

The library is quiet at this time of the morning. I quickly drop my books into the returns pile and head for the fiction shelves. It doesn't take me long to find several books by my favourite authors. My feet haven't recovered from the walk yet, so I amble towards the couches in the corner to rest for a bit. I drop my bag by my feet, and slowly attempt to lower myself onto the couch. It's a lot lower than I thought and it takes me a few goes.

"Here, let me help." A firm hand grasps my elbow, and another is placed across my back, gently guiding me to the couch below.

"Thank you," I say breathlessly, as I gaze into eyes of green and gold.

"You're welcome." He smiles, and his eyes light up, the gold flecks somehow even more vibrant. "How far along are you?" he asks, nodding towards my bump as he perches on the arm of the chair.

It crosses my mind to toy with him and pretend that I don't know what he's talking about, but my mouth won't co-operate and all I manage to say is, "Wha? Um…" I can feel my cheeks reddening with embarrassment as I stutter. "Nearly um, full term." I tilt my head to the side, allowing my hair to fall across my face.

"Wow, and you're still walking here every day?" he asks.

"Um, yeah. I love to read." Why could I not be better at this?

*He's just a guy and you're about to burst. Relax. He's not hitting on you.*

I purse my lips as I realise what he just said. "Wait, how did you know I come here every day?"

He chuckles. "Sorry, that probably seemed a bit rude. I work here. I'm usually pushing the book returns trolley when you come in." He directs my eyes to the rickety old trolley standing only a metre away. *How did I miss that?*

"Oh," I say, wishing that I didn't have a memory like a sieve. Though I'm sure, had I seen him, I would've remembered. I peek through my hair, trying to catch another glimpse of his exquisite face. Never have I ever seen a man so striking before. Not in real life, anyway. I study his face, hoping to etch it in my mind for later. He has a strong, square jaw with a dusting of stubble. His lips are full, and soft-looking, making me want to kiss them. But it's his eyes that draw me in. Green with flecks of gold, framed with long dark lashes that put mine to shame. He wears wire-framed glasses that only accentuate them even more. He chuckles again, and I realise he's caught me staring. Flustered, I fumble with the books in my hand and they fall to the floor.

"Here, let me get those for you." He crouches down at my feet, his hand resting beside my thigh as he gathers the books in his other hand. When he hands them to me, our fingers brush against each other and I almost gasp at the jolt of warmth that flows through me. "I'd better get back to it," he says, pointing his thumb behind him where the trolley awaits his return. He holds my stare a beat before getting to his feet.

"Uh, thanks," is all I can manage to say. I quickly open one of the books on my lap so that I don't make an even bigger fool of myself.

"I'll see ya round." He saunters back to his trolley, and I can't stop my eyes from following. *God, even his walk is sexy.* He turns back towards me and gives a little wave, his lip turned up at the corner in a half-grin, as if he's just thought of something funny. My lack of confidence has me wondering if that something funny, is me.

# Chapter Three

Nathan

I don't know what it is about her, but I can't get her out of my head. The girl with the long blonde hair and eyes as blue as the sky on a summer's day. The girl who seems to carry the weight of the world on her shoulders, and a tiny life inside of her. The girl who takes my breath away every damn day that I'm here, as I watch her in silence.

I reluctantly push the trolley away from her, catching one final glimpse of the smile that lights up her eyes before her brow furrows in confusion. *Did I do something wrong? Should I go back to her? Or perhaps I should leave her alone.*

I tried my best to stay away. I really did. I mean, she's carrying another man's child, I have no right to go after her. But when I saw her struggling, I had no choice. I had to go to her, and that's when I realised that her eyes, though vibrant, have a sadness in their depths. A sadness that I want to take away. Is it so wrong to want to make her smile? To make her happy?

Who am I kidding? Of course it's wrong. She belongs to someone else, and I'm not the kind of guy who leads women astray. Not intentionally, anyway. They all know exactly where they stand when they take me home. Shaking my head, I try to convince myself that there's nothing special about her. That I've built her up in my mind to be something more than she is.

I turn my attention back to the mundane task of shelving books. *You need this job, don't get distracted,* I reprimand myself. Three months on the inside doesn't exactly give you ample opportunities for jobs, and I'm lucky to have had this one handed to me. I can't be seen to be slacking off or they'll send me packing.

Still, my concentration is shot and I have to drag myself away from where she sits. Out of sight, out of mind, or so they say. Now that I've spoken to her, though, all I want to do is go back and ask her more questions so I can hear the musical tones of her voice again. I can't help wondering what other sounds I could get her to make, given the chance…

"Excuse me? Do you work here?" a wavering voice asks from behind, putting an end to my little daydream.

I cough to clear my throat. "Yes, what can I do for you?" I ask the little old lady who is stooped over so far she looks as though she may topple over at any moment.

"I'm looking for the craft books. My granddaughter is coming to visit, and I wanted to find something fun we could do together." She smiles up at me and reminds me of my own grandmother and the afternoons

I would spend helping her to paint ceramic pots for her garden.

"What a lovely idea. Right this way." I offer her my elbow as I was always taught to do, and lead her down to the other end of the library. "Here you go," I say, pointing at the rows of books. "You should be able to find something you want here."

"You're a good boy," she says, gently patting my arm before turning her attention to the shelves.

When I go to leave, I see the blonde girl making her way towards me. Her eyes are cast down at the floor, one hand resting on her belly and the other clutching her bag of books to her side. Without even thinking, my feet begin walking over to her.

"You off already?" I ask when I'm close enough. She gasps and holds her hand to her chest. "Sorry, I didn't mean to scare you." I grin at her, hoping to see that smile of hers one last time.

"Um, yeah." She brushes her hair behind her ear, giving me a better view of her face. Her alabaster skin looks as smooth as marble and I have to stop myself from reaching out and running a finger down her cheek. She doesn't wear any make-up, and she doesn't need to, either. She has a natural beauty that radiates from her, especially when her perfectly pink, rosebud lips curl into a smile. What I wouldn't do for that smile.

"Will I see you tomorrow?" I ask hopefully.

"Yeah, maybe." And there it is. That smile. It's only brief, but it's there, and that's all I need to get through the rest of the day.

# Chapter Four

Jess

*He wants to see me again.* At least, I think he does. That's what he was meaning, wasn't it? When he asked if he would see me tomorrow? I mean, I'm no expert at reading guys, but he did approach me. Twice. That's got to be a good thing, right?

*He works there, remember? It's his job to be nice.*

My mind is running around in circles, trying to make sense of what happened in there. I've only ever had one boyfriend, so reading guys is in no way my expertise. I need someone with a little more experience to tell me what they think. I stop at the corner and weigh up my options. I could walk back to my parents' place and go crazy trying to figure him out, or I could go and see Sarah and Kelly and get their take on the hot librarian.

It's not a difficult decision. Ten minutes later, I'm sitting at their table, telling them about my run-in.

"Ooh, it's just like a scene from a movie," Sarah gushes. "The hot librarian sees a damsel in distress and comes to her rescue." The look on her face is priceless. Kelly and I exchange a knowing look. Of the three of us, Sarah is the one who still holds out hope that her Prince Charming will arrive and whisk her off into the sunset. "It's just so romantic."

"Or stalkerish," Kelly adds. "I mean, the guy obviously watches you to have known that you walk there every day. It's either really sweet, or super creepy."

"Come on, Kelly, don't be so negative! He could be a real sweetheart."

"Yeah," she draws the word out slowly. "I'm just saying, she should be cautious."

I drop my head into my hands. "You guys were supposed to help me, not confuse me even more."

"Okay, well, did you happen to get a name?"

*Why didn't I think of that?*

I know he had a nametag on, I remember seeing it. I just don't remember paying attention to what it said. I was too busy staring into his beautiful eyes.

"Earth to Jess." Kelly clicks her fingers in front of my face and I blink before turning my head to look at her. "Did you get a name?" she says again.

"Oh, no."

"I know! We can google it!" Sarah jumps up excitedly, retrieving her phone from her bag.

"How are we meant to google him without a name?"

"Ah, duh. We can look up the library and see if they have their staff pictures on there."

"Oh! That's a great idea!"

She pulls up the website and within minutes she has found the staff directory. Handing me the phone, she says, "Scroll through, and see if you can find him."

It's not hard to spot him. Apparently, he's the only guy who works there. "There, that's him." I hold the phone out for them to see. "Nathan Frost."

"Nathan Frost?" Kelly demands.

"That's what it says," I say, concern building at the tone of her voice.

"No. Uh-uh. He's bad news. Don't go there, Jess." She shakes her head and begins to tap her foot up and down on the floor.

Sarah grabs the phone from my hand and peers at the photo.

"Why, what's wrong with him?" I stammer, picking at one of my nails.

"He's definitely a looker. I can see why you like him," Sarah says. "He doesn't look all that bad to me."

"Looks aren't everything. Jess, he's been to prison. You don't want that around your baby."

Both Sarah and I gasp. "Prison?" I whisper.

"Yeah. You remember earlier in the year, there was a guy who punched that cop? That was him!"

"Are you sure?" Sarah asks. "That's a pretty serious thing to accuse him of."

"Of course I'm sure! Are you forgetting my mum works on reception at the cop shop? She warned me to stay away from him *and* his brother. They've been in and out of trouble. They're not good guys. I'm sorry,

Jess." She pulls my hands into hers, and it's then that I notice the blood. I'd been picking the skin around my nail and hadn't even realised.

"Oh, Jess! Let me get a Band-Aid." Sarah jumps up from her seat and darts out the door. When she returns, she has a first aid kit in her arms.

"Sorry, I didn't mean to," I whisper. I can't seem to get my eyes to stay focused on anything while she cleans me up. All I can think about is how much I want Kelly to be wrong.

# Chapter Five

Nathan

I've turned into a woman. That's the only explanation. I may as well hand over my man-card right now. I stare at the three shirts strewn across my bed while I grab a fourth and see if that one works better. I'm not even sure what look it is that I'm going for, all I know is that it must be perfect. Is this what girls do every time they go out? If so, it's no wonder it takes them so long to get ready.

In the end, I settle on a dark-blue, button-up shirt and jeans, with the only pair of shoes I own. A spritz of cologne and a quick trim of the unruly scruff on my chin that seems to get longer every time I look in the mirror, and I'm just about ready to go. I run my hand through my hair, bringing it to rest on one side. That'll have to do.

Grabbing my keys from the counter, I head out the door and down the road. Is it wrong that I'm nervous and excited to see her again? We've barely spoken, but I feel like we've got this connection already. I've never felt anything like this before. Girls have always been a bit of a distraction for me, something to pass the time. I've never wanted anything more than that before. Not until I laid eyes on her.

Not that I have any right to go after her. What's she going to want with a guy like me? When she finds out that I've been to jail, she'll run for the hills, and who could blame her? No new mother is going to want a jailbird around their child, especially one who's been done for assault. I shake my head in frustration, rubbing my hand down the length of my jaw.

"Damn it, Noah!" I curse under my breath. If only he'd listened to me, things could have been different. I never would have hit that cop, and wouldn't know the inside of a jail cell intimately.

I take a deep breath in through my nose and exhale in a huff through my mouth. *You made your decision*, I remind myself. *You could have walked away.*

Yeah. I could have. And then what? Noah would have been the one on the inside, or worse, and I'd still have been the one to blame. I've seen the way Mum looks at me. Like I'm the bad son. The disappointment.

If I could turn back the clock and change things, I would. I know she blames me for the death of my father. Hell, I blame me too. But I've worked my ass off to make her proud of me. To be the son she wishes I was. I kept good grades, never broke curfew, or took one step out of place.

Noah, though. He's been in and out of trouble more times than I can remember. Two years my senior, and yet, I'm the one who has had to bail him out time and time again. It's me he calls, not her. He can't have her thinking that he's less than perfect.

Noah, the son who can do no wrong.

Noah, the addict. The petty thief. The thug.

I honestly don't know how she can't know. Even I've heard the stories around town. *Watch out for those Frost Brothers, they're trouble. Rotten eggs, the both of them.* It makes me wonder if she just turns a blind eye. She can barely stand to look at me most days, but Noah gets her undivided attention and love.

I get it. I'm a constant reminder of what could have been. I don't really remember much about him, but I've seen the pictures. I look exactly like him. And I'm the reason he's dead. She's made damn sure that I know that.

I was three years old when it happened. I had been playing out in the yard with Noah, as Mum and Dad watched us from the porch. We were throwing a ball back and forth, or trying to, at least. Noah had thrown it too high and it had gone over the fence. Me, being the hyperactive toddler that I was, ran straight out the gate and onto the road to retrieve it. Dad had run out after me, throwing me to the footpath, out of the way of oncoming traffic. I'd barely left his arms when the truck hit him, sending him flying. That's what I remember of him. Not his laugh, or his hugs. No. What I remember is seeing his lifeless body soar through the air and land with a thud on the hard concrete.

I remember crying because I'd grazed my arm and skinned my knee as my body scraped along the footpath. And I remember Mum, her face twisted into a look of sheer agony as she cradled my father's head in her lap.

It was the neighbours who picked me up and tended to my wounds. They watched me and Noah while Mum went off in the ambulance with Dad. They were the ones to console us when she came home without him. We never even got to say goodbye.

That was the last day that my mother had shown any interest in my life at all. She never hugged me again, and barely acknowledged my existence except to berate me or find something else to blame me for. She sought solace in the bottom of a bottle, and the tiny amount of compassion she had left inside, was saved for Noah.

Noah, my selfish brother, who doesn't even appreciate her love.

# Chapter Six

Jess

My library bag sits there, taunting me. I want nothing more than to go and see Nathan, but Kelly's warning plays over and over in my head.

*He's bad news.*

*He's been to prison.*

*Stay away from him and his brother.*

I can't quite get my head around the fact that we're talking about the same person. Nathan doesn't seem like the type to go around punching people for no reason. Not that there's ever a good reason to punch a cop. You just don't do that.

*But he did.*

A long sigh escapes my lips as I pace the length of the living room. My eyes continue to stare at the bag longingly. Is it really going to hurt? It's a public place, what could he possibly do to me?

I know I shouldn't, but I can't resist the pull. I have to see him again. Just one more time, and then I'll be too busy with bubs to worry about him anymore. Yes.

One more tiny glimpse into those perfect seas of green will rid me of my obsession, I'm sure of it. At least, that's what I tell myself anyway. Empty promises are nothing new to me. *Just one more chance. He won't hurt me again, just this once.* I became a pro at lying to myself long before I got pregnant.

I throw the straps of my bag over my shoulder and hurry out the door before I can change my mind.

The fresh air helps to calm my nerves as I waddle down the familiar streets. A group of children playing in the park catch my attention, and I find myself subconsciously rubbing my belly with a smile on my face.

"That'll be us one day soon," I say softly. I get a nudge in response and I giggle. "You like that idea, huh?"

"They say talking to yourself is the first sign of madness."

I look up, startled. I hadn't noticed anyone else on the path.

"Sorry, didn't mean to scare you. I'm Noah." He holds his hand out to me.

"Ah, Jess," I sputter, cautiously shaking his hand. "And I wasn't talking to myself." I motion to my bump.

He chuckles. "Yeah, I noticed. I was just joking. You mind if I walk with you?" he asks as he falls into step beside me.

"Um, sure. Okay." This is awkward. Who is this guy and why does he seem so familiar? There's just something about him that has me on edge.

"Where you headed?"

"Nowhere," I lie. "Just getting some fresh air."

"Oh. I thought you might've been going to the library." He points at my bag and I silently curse as I realise that I'm carrying a bag full of books that clearly have the words *Property of the Public Library* stamped on them.

"Oh, ah... yeah," I mumble as I begin to feel the heat rise in my cheeks.

"I'm going there too."

"You are?" I ask, unable to hide my surprise as I take in his tatty jeans and tatted up arms. *Never judge a book...*

"Yeah." He leans down to whisper in my ear. "I can read."

"I didn't mean..."

His laugh stops me mid-sentence. "I'm just fooling around. Lighten up." We carry on walking in an awkward silence. As we reach the corner before the Library, I see Nathan coming from the adjacent street. My heart leaps into my throat and begins to race and I can't help the grin that forms on my lips.

"I see you know my brother," Noah says, grabbing my arm to lead me across the road. "Bro!"

# Chapter Seven

Nathan

*Damn it! Why does he have to come to my work? How many times do I have to have this conversation with him?* I look up from the pavement, a scowl already plastered on my face. He only ever comes here when he wants something.

"What do you want, Noah?" I growl.

"Is that any way to speak to your big brother and his friend?" He shifts to the side and that's when I see her. The blonde from the library is standing beside Noah, looking uncomfortable. My eyes glide over her, landing on the place where he grips her arm and I fight to contain my rage. I shove my hands in my pockets to keep them from balling into fists.

Turning my attention back to my brother, I ask again. "What do you want?"

He lets go of her arm and slaps his hand down on my shoulder, shielding her from me, but not before I see her rubbing her arm.

"I just wanted to see if you could spot me a twenty, little bro?" he grins, but I can see the look in his eyes. He's in need of a hit.

"It's only Wednesday, man. Didn't you get paid yesterday?"

"Yeah, but you know how it is. Come on, man. I need it." His grip on my shoulder tightens, and I fight to stay calm. When I glare at him, his cool demeanour falters and he starts to pick at his skin. He's gotten pretty good at hiding it from others, but he can't hide it from me. I've seen it too many times.

When he loosens his hold, I sigh, knowing I can't turn him down. Fishing out a couple of crumpled notes, I hand him forty dollars, my hand gripping it long enough to make him look at me. I lean in close to his ear. "You can have this, on the condition that you leave *her* alone."

"What's the matter, baby brother? Don't wanna share your toys? Sharing is caring." He grins cockily, trying to wrench the money from my grip.

I clench my jaw tight, speaking slowly and clearly, making sure he hears me. "I mean it, Noah. You stay away."

"Okay, okay. Chill, man. She's all yours." He turns back to her. "Catch ya later, Jess."

*Jess.*

She offers a small wave, but I can see that she's relieved to see him go.

"Are you okay? Did he hurt you?" I ask, my eyes sweeping over her as I move closer.

"Um… yeah, I'm fine," she whispers, and I'm scared that I'm going to lose her before I've even had her in my arms. *Damn it, Noah!*

"So… um… how do you know Noah?"

"Oh, I don't. He just kinda started walking with me back there. I didn't want to be rude."

"Good."

"Good?"

*Shit, this isn't a conversation I want to be having right now.*

"Yeah. He's… you should probably stay away from him." I run my hand through my hair, wondering if she's heard the stories already.

"Funny you should say that." She looks at me, not with fear, but curiosity. "My friends said the same thing about you."

*Shit.*

"Oh." I should've known. "What did they say?"

"That you've been to prison. That you hit a cop." She glances down to the ground then back up at me with concern in her eyes. "Is it true?" she whispers.

*Here goes nothing.*

"Yeah, it is." I shuffle my feet side-to-side, waiting for her to tell me to leave her alone.

Instead, she asks, "Why'd you do it?"

I'm stunned. Of all the people who've found out about my past, she is the first to actually ask for my side of the story.

"My brother, Noah, I don't know if you noticed, but he's an addict. He's been in trouble a lot and the last time he went to court they told him he'd go away if he so much as sneezed the wrong way." I take a deep breath, raking my hand through my hair again. "He didn't listen though. He never does. He was fooling around in town one night and things got a bit heated between him and some friends. He rang me to come get him, but by the time I got there, a cop had already shown up. His friends had all bailed and Noah was getting mouthy with him. As soon as I laid eyes on him, I could see he was tweaking. So, I did the first thing I could think of to turn the attention away from him."

"So, you hit a cop. You went to jail, so that your brother wouldn't have to?"

"Yeah. I knew that if he went down for it, Mum would never recover. He's... I don't know, her favourite, I guess."

"Parents aren't meant to have favourites."

"Yeah, well mine does."

She reaches out and touches my arm. "I'm sorry, Nathan. That must've been really hard for you."

Something about her touch has my eyes watering, and I have to turn my head away so she doesn't see. "Yeah, well... He's my brother," is all I can say. "I understand if you don't want me around."

"Nathan, none of this is your fault. I think what you did was sweet. A little unorthodox maybe, but sweet all the same."

It's been a long time since anyone has given a shit about how I feel. Or even taken the time to listen to what I have to say. Really listen, you know? And then this angel shows up from out of the blue, with her blonde halo and bright blue eyes, and brings everything up to the surface. Everything that I've pushed deep down. Damn those tears. I push my thumb and forefinger under my glasses and into the corners of my eyes to stop them from falling. I can't even speak to let her know how much it means to me.

"Nathan?" she says, her grip on my arm tightening. I quickly swipe my sleeve across my eyes to remove any trace of tears before turning to face her. She has a pained look on her face, and she's clutching her stomach. "I think the baby's coming."

# Chapter Eight

Jess

*Sweet baby Jesus that hurts!* I clutch my stomach and squeeze his arm as I ride through the pain. "Nathan?" I blurt out, a little panicked. All my pre-natal lessons have gone out of my head and I suddenly have no idea what I'm meant to do. When he turns to look at me, I can see that he's been crying, but I'm too preoccupied with my own problem. "I think the baby's coming," I say instead.

"What? Are you sure?" he asks, a look of shock on his face.

"Well, no not really," I admit as the pain subsides. "I've never felt anything like that before, though."

"Should we get you to the hospital?" He drapes his arm around my shoulders and takes my hand, leading me to a bench seat in front of the library.

"I... I don't know. Maybe we should wait and see if there are any more before we do that." I manage to smile even though inside, I'm nervous as hell. That was only one contraction, how am I going to handle more of those? And don't get me started on the pushing part. That scares the shit out of me! I've been so excited about meeting my baby, that I never took into consideration all the pain I would have to go through to actually get to that point. Oh God, what if I can't do it? What if something goes wrong?

"Hey, are you okay?" Nathan asks, breaking the train wreck of thoughts racing through my mind. "You've gone white and you're breathing funny. Are you sure I shouldn't call an ambulance?"

"I... no, I'm okay. Just a little scared. I've never done this before," I say, with tears brimming.

"Do you want me to call your partner?"

"No...um...I don't have one. I mean, we're not together anymore," I whisper as I feel the start of another contraction. I squeeze his hand again, leaning forward as if I can escape the pain somehow.

"Breathe, Jess. You'll pass out if you hold your breath." I huff out the air in my lungs, not even realising I'd been holding it in. "That's it. Just breathe." He brushes a stray hair behind my ear and continues to soothe me with his voice until I'm able to sit up again.

He eases his hand out of mine, giving it a shake. "You've got some grip there."

"Sorry," I reply sheepishly. "Guess I don't know my own strength."

He chuckles, bringing my hand up to his lips and planting a kiss on my fingers. "It's no problem, don't worry about it." He places my hand on his knee, his thumb drawing slow circles, making it hard for me to concentrate on anything but the feel of his skin. "So?" he says.

"What?"

"Did you want me to call someone for you? Your parents, maybe?" I'm glad someone is thinking straight.

"Um... I don't know. They're out of town visiting my aunt. My due date isn't until next week and they thought they'd be back in time," I explain. "Sarah and Kelly will be at work so I can't call them either," I say half to myself. What am I going to do? I barely have time to think before my stomach starts to tighten again. "Shit," I hiss, my fingers automatically curling around his thigh.

"You're doing great, Jess. Just keep breathing," Nathan says, his hand firm on my back. *How does he know what I need before I do?*

"Thanks," I murmur, when the contraction subsides.

"For what?"

"Being here. I don't want to do this on my own." My voice catches in my throat as I try not to cry. I never imagined I would have to do this by myself. I had always pictured *him* by my side, but now I'm here, on the street, sitting with a guy I barely know, while my body is preparing to do something I'm not sure I'm ready to do. I don't even realise the tears have started trailing down my cheek until he wipes them away with his finger.

"Hey, come here," he says, pulling me in to his side. I feel my cheeks redden as I suddenly become all too aware of his body against mine. I know it's inappropriate of me to notice these things when I'm about to have another man's baby, but damn if his body isn't rock hard. I can feel the muscles in his shoulder flexing as he strokes his hand up and down my arm and I can't help but snuggle in closer. "You don't have to do this alone," he says softly.

God, I've never wanted to kiss someone as much as I want to kiss him right now. I tilt my head up to look into those eyes that mesmerise me. They're like a window to his soul and it dawns on me that even though he puts on a brave face, he's been hurt too. I remember that I'd seen tears in those eyes not so long ago, and it breaks my heart to think that this kind man has been misjudged too often.

Staring into those seas of green, I am overcome with emotion and without really thinking about it, I slowly begin to lean in, closing my eyes. Our lips are only a breath away when I pull back, crying out, "Ahh, fuck me!"

Nathan blinks, stunned by my outburst, and even though I'm doubled over in pain, I can see that he's trying not to laugh. I guess I can see why. It *is* kind of funny to have someone yell that in your face. I muster up a smile, even managing to giggle as the ache diminishes.

"Well, that's not something that happens every day," he says with a sexy lopsided grin. "A beautiful girl demanding such vulgar things when I haven't even taken her on a proper date." He shakes his head. "What is this world coming to?"

I slap his leg playfully. "Shut-up, I was in pain," I whine, though deep down, I'm doing a happy dance that he not only called me beautiful, but suggested that he might be interested in a date with me.

"I know, I'm sorry." He rubs my back soothingly. "How are you feeling?"

"Box of fluffies. You?" I ask sarcastically.

"Never been better." He smiles, leaning back on the seat, his arms stretched out across the back of it. When the town clock chimes, his face drops. "Shit. I'm meant to be starting work."

"Oh. Okay," I say, disappointment in my voice. I don't know why I'm surprised, we *are* sitting outside his place of work after all.

"Hang on, I'll go tell them I can't come in."

"You don't have to do that, Nathan."

"Yeah, I do. I'm not leaving you on your own." He gets to his feet. "I'll just be a minute." He turns and runs towards the doors, not even giving me a chance to respond. In all honesty, though, I'm relieved. The thought of doing this all on my own is unbearable.

"All on your lonesome again, I see," the familiar voice of Noah chimes from behind me. I can't quite put my finger on it, but something in the way he looks at me gives me the creeps.

"No, Nathan will be back, he just had to run inside for a sec," I say, hoping that I sound convincing. I can feel the beginning of another contraction and I'd rather not show him any sign of pain.

"You, ah, want some company?" he asks, taking a seat beside me anyway. His leg is pushed up against mine and I suddenly feel cornered.

"Um... I think we're going to be leaving soon." I turn towards the door, hoping to see Nathan, even though I know he only just left me.

"That's okay, this won't take long, sweetheart." He grins at me, the smell of tobacco strong on his breath. "See, I just wanted to see if you'd do something for me." He places his hand on my thigh, sending a chill up my spine.

"Like what?" I ask tightly, watching his hand while trying to breathe through the pain.

"Well, the thing is, I need some cash," he says, his grip on my thigh intensifying. "I thought you might be able to help me out."

"I...I don't have any money," I whisper as the pain in my stomach and now my thigh, increases.

"Now, I don't think that's true. A nice girl like you's gotta have some cash on her, what with a baby on the way." His voice takes on a menacing tone as his hand moves higher. I glance towards the library entrance again, desperately seeking a familiar face. "I don't want any trouble, Jess. Just hand over your wallet, and I'll leave you alone."

"I told you, I-I don't have any money," I say frantically. "Check my bag!"

"Jess!" he growls, jumping to his feet. "Don't lie to me!

# Chapter Nine

Nathan

*What the fuck?*

I round the corner to see Noah standing over Jess, his hands on her shoulders as he yells in her face. I break into a run, pulling him away from her.

"I told you to leave her alone!" I yell, dragging him to the ground. I pin him under my body. "Why do you have to ruin everything?"

"What? You actually think you've got a chance with her?" Noah scoffs. "Oh, this is priceless! Open your fucking eyes, man! She's pregnant! What you gonna do? Pretend like you haven't been to jail? Play happy families with someone else's kid?" Gripping his shirt in my fists, I glare down at him. "Oops, did I let the cat out of the bag? Didn't your *girlfriend* know you'd been to jail?"

"Go to hell, Noah! You think you're so smart, throwing that out there, well guess what? She knows everything! She knows that I went away to save *your* ass, and she doesn't care!" I pause, taking a deep breath before lowering my voice so that only he can hear me. "It's none of your fucking business what I do, or who I do it with. Now, Stay. The Fuck. Away from her, before I make you," I seethe, my hands fighting to show him how much she means to me.

"Nathan?" Her voice is tiny and laced with fear. *Oh God! How could I be so stupid? Going off at him in front of her like that? Way to show her that you're a good role model.*

It takes every ounce of my strength to turn away from my brother. When I do, I find her hunched over the bench seat, clutching her stomach as fluid runs down her legs.

"Oh shit, Jess!" I cry, running to her side, my brother all but forgotten. "We need to get you to the hospital. Now."

She nods, reaching out for my hand as she begins rocking back and forth on her heels. "Okay," she hisses through her teeth. I can't stand to see her in so much pain.

"Noah, ring an ambulance," I say calmly. Wrapping my arms around her waist, I help her perch on the seat. I glance over at Noah, who is still lying on the ground, staring in horror as Jess starts moaning, tears streaming down her face. "Noah! Ambulance!" I say louder, breaking him from his trance.

"Phone?" he asks, as he gets to his feet.

"Back pocket. Hurry, I don't think we have much time before this baby arrives." I crouch down in front of her, my hands resting on her knees. "Jess, look at me." I brush her hair away from her face, tilting her chin up. "You can do this, okay? You're doing great."

She shakes her head, her breath coming out in a moan. "I can't... I can't do this..." she mumbles, a look of sheer agony on her face. "I thought I could... but I can't." When her body practically folds in half with the pain, she whispers, "I'm scared, Nathan."

"I know you are, but, Jess? I'm gonna be right here with you, okay? We'll do it together." Somehow my words get a hint of a smile out of her and my heart almost bursts. I would do anything to take her pain away and see that smile again, the one that lights up her face. *Even in the throes of pain, she's still the most beautiful woman I've ever seen.*

"They're on the way," Noah says, handing my phone back. "Shit, is she okay?" he asks, his hands seeking the scars on his arms.

Without taking my eyes from hers, I respond, "She's doing great. You can go now, Noah. I got this."

"I... uh..." he shuffles his feet, sweeping his hand through his hair several times.

I sigh, cursing under my breath. "What do you want?"

"Have you got any more cash?" he asks, and this time has the decency to look embarrassed.

"What happened to the money I gave you?" I demand.

"It wasn't enough. Price's gone up. Assholes." *Of course it has. A junkie will pay no matter what the cost.*

I reach into my pocket and pull out another twenty. "That's all I've got."

"Thanks, man." He turns to leave, pausing beside Jess. "I'm sorry for before," he mumbles. If he could just get off the gear, I'm sure that he'd be a decent guy. I make a promise to myself to get him some help when this is all done. I've been holding onto the anger inside, blaming him for my jail stint, but in reality, he never asked me to do it. I had thought I was doing him a favour, but maybe I was just enabling him even more.

"Noah?" I call out before he gets to the corner. "Be careful."

# Chapter Ten

I can honestly say, I have never felt anything more excruciating than childbirth. Once the ambulance had arrived, and I'd convinced them to let Nathan come with me, everything went pretty fast. There was no time for an epidural. I had to do it *au naturel*. Let me just say, I have a new-found respect for my mother.

No amount of classes and information can truly prepare you for giving birth. And don't get me started on the bullshit the movies will have you believe. Two pushes and a baby is born? Please! I was pushing for a good forty-five minutes before his head finally came out. And then there's the afterbirth. I don't recall there ever being mention of that. I thought I was done and then the contractions started all over again. I'm gonna be honest here, it scared the crap out of me! Twins, was all that was floating through my head until they explained what was going on.

One thing they got right though? Once your baby is out and in your arms? You forget all about the pain. You fall instantly in love. There's no greater feeling.

James is his name. James Nathaniel Ferguson. And he's perfect.

I know people will think I'm crazy naming him after Nathan, but I don't care. He was there when I needed him, and he was fantastic. I don't think I could've done this without him. When I wanted to give up, he picked me up and pushed me through. He sponged my forehead down, held my hand while I squeezed it to death, and whispered words of encouragement. I have never met anyone like him. For all that he's been through, his support was unwavering.

"Darling?" the voice of my mother rings out from the corridor. "Oh my God!" she gasps as she enters the room, rushing to my side. "Oh, honey, he's perfect."

"Thanks, *I* think so," I say, a goofy grin on my face.

"I'm so sorry you had to do this on your own," she says with tears in her eyes. I quickly place my hand on hers.

"Mum, it's okay. I wasn't on my own. I had Nathan with me." I smile, gesturing to the other side of the room. "Nathan took care of us."

"Nathan." Dad nods his head, offering his hand. "Thanks for taking care of our baby girl."

"It was my pleasure, Sir," he says, standing. "You've got a great daughter there. She was amazing." He smiles at me, making my heart melt even more. How could anyone not love him?

"I don't doubt it. She's always been strong. Even so, I really appreciate you being here for her."

"There's nowhere else I'd rather be."

"Hmm," Mum says, her lips pursed.

"Ah… I should leave you guys to catch up. I'll come back in later, if that's okay, Jess?" He seems so nervous. It's kind of cute.

"Of course! You're always welcome," I say. "And, Nathan? Thanks. For everything."

"Don't mention it." He winks and offers a half-smile before walking out the door.

He's barely left the room before Mum pipes up. "You *do* know who that is, right? What have you gotten yourself into this time?"

Taken aback, I have no idea what to say. "I… I haven't gotten myself *into* anything, Mum. Nathan is a friend."

"You don't fool me, sweetheart. I can see it in your eyes. He's more than a friend." She frowns, smoothing her hands down her shirt. "You need to be careful who you hang out with, Jess. You're a mother now, it's not just about you and what you want."

"I can't believe you just said that," I whisper. "You were out of town, and I had no one here to help me. He could've walked away. But he didn't. He helped me get through one of the hardest things I've ever had to do in my life."

"That may be the case, but," she lowers her voice, "he's been in prison! You do know that, right?"

I sigh dramatically. "Of course I know that. But unlike other people, I don't jump to conclusions about him. He told me the whole story. He was protecting his brother. He's a good guy, Mum. Trust me."

"I just hope you know what you're doing." Her brow is creased with worry and I guess I can see why. I haven't exactly made things easy for her over the last few years.

"It's okay. I know what I'm doing. Now, would you like to hold your grandson?"

# Chapter Eleven

Nathan

There's no doubt about it. That was the single most beautiful thing I have ever seen in my life. Jess just continues to impress me. It takes a lot of strength to do something like that. To bring a new life into this world.

I would give anything to be a part of this with her. To witness her as a mother. But I know I have no right to those feelings. I know I was only here by default. You know what though? I'd do it all over again in a heartbeat.

Jess is the kind of girl you want to take home to your mother. The one you proudly hold on your arm wherever you go. How anyone could treat her so badly that she would feel that leaving while heavily pregnant was the best option, is something I can't comprehend. If she was mine, I would show her how special she was. Every. Damn. Day.

That being said, I didn't miss the looks her mother gave me. I could see in her eyes that she knew exactly who I was, and wanted me nowhere near her daughter. I can't say I blame her really. My reputation doesn't exactly scream boyfriend material.

Leaving them to their family time, I trudge down the hall and out into the air. My phone buzzes in my pocket and pulling it out, I see a message from Heath, one of Noah's 'friends'.

**Noah's flipped out.**

*Shit.* I quickly type out a response.

**Where is he? What happened?**

I'm already walking, knowing that I'll have to move fast to stop him from doing anything stupid. Again.

**Darren's. He's breaking shit. Someone called the cops.**

*Fuck!* I break out into a run. Darren lives only a few blocks away from the hospital, and I'm grateful for small mercies. If the cops get to him first, he'll go down for sure and my stint in jail would have been for nothing.

Rounding the corner, I can already see that he's drawn attention to himself as the neighbours stand around rubber-necking. There's shouting and the sound of things being smashed. Pumping my arms, I make it to the rundown house just in time to see Noah throw an old-school box TV across the lawn and into the side of the garage. Someone is screaming inside, and I don't know where to go first.

"Thank fuck you're here, man." Heath runs up to join me. "He took something, I don't know what, but it must've been laced. He's trippin' hard core."

"Where'd he get the stuff?" I ask, pacing back and forth.

"Same as always, far as I know." Heath brings his hand up to his mouth, chewing on his thumbnail. "He was jacked up when he showed up here. Smashed Darren a good one, right on the nose. Blood everywhere. His mum's fuckin' spewing."

*Fuck!* "She the one who called the cops?"

"Come on, man, you know better than that. We ain't no snitches." He swipes his fist across his nose, sniffing loudly. "She's just pissed he's messin her place up. Sent him outside where she didn't have to worry about him trashin' her stuff." He throws his thumb over his shoulder towards the street. "One of these dickheads made the call."

*Fuck it.* "Thanks, Heath. I'll get it sorted." I clamp my hand on his shoulder. "See if you can get these people to go back home."

"No worries, man." He jaunts off down the drive, waving his arms at everyone as he yells, "Nothin' to see here!"

Turning my attention back to Noah, I make my way to the back of the house. "Noah!" I call out, stepping around the corner. Holding my hands out in front of me in submission, I edge closer to him. "Noah, you need to calm down. Talk to me. What's going on?"

"Can't you see them?" he screams, spittle spraying from his mouth as he stares straight through me with a crazed look in his eyes. "They're fucking everywhere!"

"What are?" I ask, keeping my eyes glued to him as I take another step closer.

"The demons! They're trying to get me!" His head snaps back to the garage, a look of pure terror on his face. "Leave me the fuck alone!" he screams, scraping his hands down his face, leaving red marks and a few drops of blood. "Leave me alone!" He drags his eyes away, searching for something else to throw. The yard is filled with broken appliances and old furniture, like some kind of death-pit for household goods. Darren's dad is a bit of a hoarder and hates to throw things away, and everything winds up out on the lawn. I'd say he is probably regretting that right now.

An old office chair is the next thing to go. He picks it up by the backrest and hurls it at the same spot on the garage where a small pile of smashed glass and equipment is slowly building.

"Noah," I say with as much authority as I can muster. "Noah, look at me." I step into his line of sight. "Look at me."

His eyes dart back and forth from the garage to me.

"Look at me, Noah."

"Nathan?" he says, confused.

"Yes, Noah. It's me. You're going to be okay. Just stop throwing things. You're scaring people." I wave my arm out towards the crowd still gathered on the street.

"You're one of them?" His eyes widen. Stumbling backwards, he trips on a lawn chair, sending him sprawling. When he gets to his feet, he turns his gaze to me, his eyes now narrowed into slits. "I always knew you were the devil." He picks up the handle of an old garden fork and swinging it above his head, charges right at me.

# Chapter Twelve

Jess

"Please go to sleep." I sit on the edge of the hospital bed, bouncing James on my lap, willing him to give in and close his eyes. After a day full of napping, he has decided that 2AM is milk time and no matter how hard I try, I can't seem to get him to latch on properly or to get enough to soothe his little tummy.

"Everything okay in here?" one of the nurses asks as she pokes her head through the door. She has a crop of curly grey hair atop her head and reminds me a little of Mrs Doubtfire.

"He won't sleep." I sniff, ducking my head down so she can't see my tears. "I think he's really hungry, but it hurts too much. It's like broken glass is being sucked out of me. I don't think I can do it anymore."

"When was the last time he ate?" She steps in, closing the door behind her and rubbing a soothing hand across my back.

Peering up at the clock on the wall, I say, "About fifteen minutes ago. And then about half an hour before that." I pull him into my body, inhaling his sweet baby scent. "I don't know how to do this."

"You're doing just fine. Some babies are hungrier than others, and this big fella is probably just trying to bring your milk in faster." She holds her hands out. "May I?"

With a nod, I carefully place him in her arms, watching her rock him with more vigour than I'd been doing.

"Sometimes a bit of wind can get caught, and their little bodies can't quite expel it on their own. You have to give them a helping hand." She pushes him further up on her shoulder, his legs scrunched up and cupped in her hand. "That's it, let it out," she says, patting his bottom while walking around the room.

"You make it look so easy." Not even 24 hours and I'm already feeling like a failure as a parent. "I wish I knew what I was doing."

"I've had years of practice, my dear. You'll get the hang of it. Don't worry." She smiles warmly which somehow helps me to relax. "Why don't you lie down and get some rest? I can take the wee fella for a few hours so you can get some sleep. It'll all feel easier with some rest."

"Um… I don't know…" I would really love some sleep, but the idea of some stranger taking my baby away for a few hours doesn't sit well with me.

"He'll be fine, I promise." She crosses to the other side of the room. "It'll only be for a little while, and then I'll bring him back to you for feeding."

"I guess… maybe just an hour would be nice…"

She looks at me sympathetically. "It's okay to ask for help. It doesn't make you a bad mum. Babies can feel when you're upset or stressed and that can make them anxious too. Get some rest, you'll see. It will make you feel so much better."

She has a point. It's been a big day and I'm absolutely exhausted. Having Mum and Dad here most of the day and then Sarah and Kelly too, I barely had any time to rest. Climbing back under the sheets, I nod my head. "Okay, thank you."

James has already calmed down immensely, and seems rather comfortable in her arms as she carries him out to the nurses' station. Maybe I am a little too wound up. I kept hoping that Nathan would come back to see us, but he never did. At least, I don't think he did. I wouldn't put it past my mother, or Kelly for that matter, to try and persuade him to leave me alone. I'll have to show her that he's not who she thinks he is. I know the talk around town doesn't paint him in a good light, but I've seen first-hand what kind of man he is. Sure, he's made some mistakes in his life, but who hasn't? I'm no stranger to fuck-ups. Lord knows I've made my fair share. James' father was one of them. Not that I regret having James. No, he's the one good thing that came out of that godforsaken relationship.

What I do regret is the way I let him treat me. The way I let him control me so that I felt I had no one to turn to. I regret giving him so much power over me.

I don't think Nathan would ever treat me that way. He's too kind-hearted. I see it in the way he jumped right in there with me, not knowing what to expect, but doing it anyway. He could've left me with the paramedics, but he didn't. He stayed and held my hand through the whole thing. He's like my own personal knight in shining armour.

I only hope my family didn't scare him off for good.

## Chapter Thirteen

Nathan

Blinking my eyes a few times, I'm blinded by the stark white light above me.

*Where the hell am I?*

Craning my neck to look around, I am hit with a sharp pain in my head. *Son of a bitch! What the hell is going on?*

I try to sit up, but the pain extends from my ear, down the length of my neck, and across my chest. Inhaling a raspy breath, I search my memory for any clues as to what has happened.

*Noah.*

Of course. It's always Noah. Flashbacks of his drug addled melt-down bounce around in my head. The last thing I remember is him charging me, and then excruciating pain. He'd jumped me. The son of a bitch jumped me!

Feeling the anger boiling beneath my skin, I try once more to sit up. *I'm in the hospital. The fucker put me in the hospital!*

Ignoring the pain throbbing throughout my body, I fumble my hand on the table beside me, trying to locate my glasses. They've seen better days, that's for sure. Shoving the warped frames onto my face, I twist side-to-side, finding myself in a room of my own. A small window offers up a view of the grounds outside, and the darkened sky makes me wonder how long I've been in here. An IV line is hooked into the back of my hand, pumping God knows what into my body, and there appears to be cuts and bruises along both arms.

Bringing my hands to my face, I feel around for more damage. Swollen lumps have formed around both eyes and they're tender to touch. Above my left ear is a bandage, and my hair is plastered to my head. There's a ringing in my ear too, and my nose is throbbing to the beat of my heart, making me think it may be broken.

*How the hell did he do this much damage? Didn't I fight back? Didn't anyone try to stop him?*

"Ah, I see you're awake now, Mr Frost." An officer steps into the room with a cup of coffee in hand. "I'm Officer Delaney. I just need to take a statement from you, if you're up to it." He's smirking and it takes me a few minutes to realise this is the same cop I'd hit not so long ago.

*Shit.*

"Where's Noah?" I croak, hoping to get some information, and buying myself more time. "Is he here?"

"He's been detained down at the station. You're lucky you're not there with him. Disturbing the peace and all that." He saunters over to the chair in the corner of the room, making himself comfortable. Flipping open his notebook, he pulls a pen from his jacket and holds it at the ready. "Now, in your own words, tell me what happened this afternoon."

"Wait," I shake my head. "He's been detained? He's not here?" I screw my face up in confusion. *Shouldn't he be in the hospital with me?*

"No, he's not here. Like I said, he's down at the station awaiting a tox screen and a psych evaluation." Leaning forward, his elbows resting on his knees, he taps his pen on the notebook. "Now. In your own words, Mr Frost."

With my hand on my brow, I take a deep breath, struggling to come up with any way out of dropping Noah in deep shit. A tox screen will show that he was high as a kite, and I don't hold much hope for the psych test. Especially if he's still got it in his system. What had he called me? The devil?

"Look, Officer, can we do this another time? My head is killin' me."

"You know that's not how this works. You can't cover for him forever, Nathan. He's going to get caught eventually."

My head shoots up at his words, instantly sending a jolt of agony through my body.

"What? You didn't think I knew that's what you were doing? Come on, what do you take me for?"

The door to my room creeps open and a woman pops her head in. "I thought I could hear voices in here." She steps in, taking hold of my chart and skimming the pages. "How are you feeling, Mr Frost?" Her cool hand grasps my wrist as she measures my pulse.

"Ah, yeah… I feel like shit, to be honest." I muster a weary smile. "My head's pounding."

Pursing her lips, she looks to the corner of the room, eyeing the man in uniform. "Mr Frost needs to rest. I'm sure whatever you need him for can wait until the morning." Turning back to me, she smiles. "I'll see if I can get you some pain relief."

"Thank you that would be great."

She walks back to the door, holding it open with a look of contempt at Officer Delaney. "After you."

With a sigh, he gets to his feet. "Don't think this is over. I'll be back in the morning, and I *will* get your statement."

# Chapter Fourteen

Jess

What is it about hospitals that make it so hard to sleep? Is it just the unfamiliar bed, or the fact that you can hear voices down the corridor no matter what the time is? I shouldn't really complain, I somehow managed to scrape in two almost solid hours of sleep before my body insisted that I get out of bed and find my baby.

My baby.

No matter how many times I said it, those words still felt strange in my mouth. All through my pregnancy I had waited for that feeling to finally sink in, and assumed that once I held him in my arms, I'd feel it – that maternal instinct. That was not the case. Yes, I loved him as soon as I saw him, but when was it going to feel real, and not like some kind of weird dream? When was that instinctual mothering urge meant to kick in? Breastfeeding was proving to be much harder than I'd anticipated. Who'd have thought it could be so hard to get a baby to latch on? I thought it was meant to be second nature. Apparently, I missed the memo on that one.

Swinging my legs over the edge of the bed, I shuffle forward, my jiggly jelly-belly wobbling about. Yet another thing they neglect to tell you about. It may sound silly, but I had envisaged my stomach bouncing back to something a little less bulgy, and a little more... flat. No one told me I'd still look pregnant!

I poke a finger into the squidgy flesh of my belly, watching as it disappears up to my knuckle. How the hell I was meant to squeeze into my pre-pregnancy pants was beyond me.

With a sigh, I pull myself upright, the tender ache between my legs a constant reminder of what my body has endured. I make my way to the door, easing it open and blinking my eyes a little as I adjust to the light of the hallway.

The nurses' station is right across from my room. I've barely stepped foot out into the hall before a nurse is by my side.

"Is everything okay?"

"Yeah, everything is fine. I can't sleep, so I thought I'd see if James needed feeding yet." I plaster a smile on my face, hoping she won't see the fear in my eyes.

"I'll go and see if he's awake. Brenda took him down to the family room not long ago. Would you like me to bring you something to drink? Hot chocolate? Tea?"

My stomach makes an involuntary grumble at the mere mention of it. With a chuckle, I place my hands over my belly. "Yes please. Hot chocolate would be perfect, thank you."

"Not a problem. You head back in and I'll be back with that shortly."

I begin my shuffle dance once more as I venture back into my room. Instead of climbing into bed, I opt for the cushy chair in the corner, hoping it will help with the breastfeeding.

"Knock knock," the nurse's voice rings out. "Here's your hot chocolate. I'll just pop it on the tray for you here." She sets it down and pulls the tray round to my side. "Are you ready to try again with James?"

I hesitate a fraction of a beat, before answering with a nod.

"Would you like me to give you a hand this time?" She looks at me with sympathy in her eyes, and I have to bite my lip to stop the tears from forming.

"Mmhmm." I nod again with a little cough to clear my throat. "That would be good, thanks."

"No problem. I'll be right back." She pats my hand affectionately before leaving me to myself.

Grabbing a pillow from the bed, I lay it across my lap, a loose thread catching my eye. Without a thought, I hold it between my thumb and finger, the pillow case in my other hand, determined to remove the thread that could potentially wrap around my little man's fingers. A swift yank and the thread is gone. Huh. Was that what I'd been waiting for? The urge to protect my son?

A snuffly cry from the hall draws me from my thoughts. James is here. My heart feels as though it might swell to twice its size at hearing his sounds that already seem so familiar to me.

"Here she is," the nurse coos to him as she walks in, bouncing him in her arms.

Unbuttoning my shirt, I push the fabric to one side, exposing my swollen breast. *Please let him latch on this time.*

As soon as he is in my arms, he lets out a tiny cry, almost as if he has missed me. It's impossible to keep the smile from my face as I peer down at his beautiful features.

"Do you want to try and get him on by yourself so I can see?" The nurse has perched on the edge of the bed, her hands clasped on her lap.

"Uh, okay." Taking hold of my tender skin, I gingerly lead his mouth towards me. The sting is instant. "Ahhhh," I hiss, closing my eyes through the pain.

"He's not on properly, Jess. That's why it's hurting you." She quickly sits forward, her hands poised near his head. "May I?"

"Mmhmm."

With nimble fingers, she pulls him off me, much to his disgust. With one hand on the back of his head and one firmly on me, she positions him in line, then with a swift motion, she has him on and suckling before I can even say anything. He is doing it! He is actually feeding!

The pain subsides as I watch him in awe, his tiny fist clenched on my finger. Tears prick my eyes at the sheer beauty of it. "He's doing it," I whisper, looking back up at her with a goofy grin. "Thank you."

"It's my pleasure."

With his full tummy, James fell into a milk-drunk sleep. They'd shown me how to wrap him in a cocoon-type fashion; apparently they like that because it reminds them of the womb. He seems content, so who am I to argue?

I somehow managed to get him down in his crib without disturbing him, and then spent the next ten minutes staring at him. Such time-wasters, these little cherubs of joy.

My eyes wander to the window outside, it's beginning to lighten up out there. Daylight already. I've only had two hours of sleep, and I doubt I'll get any more for a while. There is no telling how long James will be asleep for, and I really want to have a shower. I don't want to be a sweaty mess if Nathan shows up to visit us.

Nathan. My saviour.

What happened to him yesterday? I was sure he'd said he'd be back. Not that I can blame him for staying away. A single mother with a new-born baby aren't exactly the kind of company young, single guys like to keep. That being said, I find myself holding out hope that we will see him again, and soon.

## Chapter Fifteen

Nathan

A dull throb in my head along with the faint glimmer of sun on my face, wakes me from my sleep. It only takes a minute to remember where I am and why.

*Damn it, Noah! Why did you have to go and ruin everything?*

I fumble with the sheets, throwing them off me as if they're offensive. Swinging my legs over the side of the bed, I attempt to stand, but the pain in my head intensifies and I fall back with a hiss. After taking a few calming breaths, I try again, only slower this time. So far, so good.

I catch a glimpse of myself in the mirror as I move around in search of a bathroom. I'm shocked to see the black and blue surrounding both eyes. Moving closer, I lift my hand to my face, gently brushing my fingers over the abrasions adorning my forehead and cheeks. My nose looks as though it's twisted on a different angle and a cut sits on the bridge, right between my eyes. Son of a bitch broke my nose! No wonder I was finding it so hard to breathe.

"Not a pretty picture, is it?" Officer Delaney steps into the room, his notepad at the ready.

"D'you sleep here or something? Bit early for house calls, isn't it?"

"You know why I'm here, Nathan. I'm not going to go away until I have your statement. Just a few words from you, and I can disappear. Believe me, I don't want to be here either." He rubs a hand around the back of his neck, and it's then that I notice the dark circles under his eyes.

"Jesus, you did sleep here, didn't you? What did you think I was going to do? Make a getaway?"

He looks at me with one eyebrow raised, as if to say *I wouldn't put it past you.*

I guess I'm going to have to get this over with. I'd barely slept last night, trying to come up with a solution that didn't end up with Noah being arrested. There were too many witnesses this time though. Not to mention the results of the tox screen, which I'm sure they've already seen. For the first time, I don't think I can save him from himself.

"Okay, what do you want to know?" I ask with a sigh, easing my aching body down onto the corner of the bed.

"Talk me through the events yesterday. Where you were, what time, who was with you, that sort of thing."

Clearing my throat, I begin. "Ah, I had been here with a friend for most of the day. I got a text around three from Heath, saying I needed to get over to Darren's."

"Mmhmm. What happened next?" He barely lifts his head as he continues to scrawl down every little thing I say.

"I ran to Darren's place. There were people out on the street, watching."

"What were they watching?"

Squeezing my eyes shut, I tried one last time to think of something, anything that could make this go away.

"Nathan?"

"They were watching Noah." The words came out on a breath, as if saying them louder would make it all the more true. "He was…" I glance out the window, hating myself for what I was about to do. "He was throwing stuff. Scaring people."

"He was throwing things at people?"

"No! God no, he wouldn't do that. Even under… He just wouldn't do that, okay?" I stare at him, waiting for his nod. "He was throwing things around the yard. At the garage, mainly."

"And why was he doing that?"

"You're really going to make me do this, aren't you?" I look down at my hands, wondering how we got to this point. His silence confirms my question. "He was seeing things. Demons."

"And *were* there demons?"

The snicker is out of my mouth before I could stop it. "You'd love that, wouldn't you? Get us both locked up for being crazy?"

"I'm just trying to get the facts."

"No. There weren't any demons. Just me, and right about now, I'm as close as you can be to being one."

"What happened next?"

"He came at me. He said I was the devil." My eyes drift back to the window. "I guess he was right."

# Chapter Sixteen

Jess

"Has he been in to see you yet?" Sarah drags a seat to my bedside so she can peer in on James while he sleeps. "God, I just wanna squish him!"

"I hope you mean James, and not Nathan." I grin, playfully swatting her shoulder with the plush rabbit she'd bought for us. "James is definitely squishable. Nathan, however..." My mind drifts off as I picture those brilliant emerald eyes of his.

"Look at you, all doe-eyed! I don't care what Kelly says, he sounds like a real sweetheart from what you've told me."

"At least someone agrees with me." I sigh. "Mum certainly doesn't approve. And you know Dad will end up siding with her eventually."

"So what if he's been to prison? It was what? Three months? *And* it was to protect his brother. There's something noble about that. Don't ya think?"

"Yeah, I do. You should've seen him yesterday, Sarah. I don't think I could've done it without him. He really looked after me. It was so sweet."

"I bet he could look after you good and proper too, if you get my meaning," she says with a wink.

I can't contain my giggle. "I don't think anyone could miss that meaning, Sarah. And yes, I'm sure he could. Here's hoping I get a chance to find out." I cross my fingers and hold them up to the sky with a silent *please.*

"Seriously though, I'm so sorry none of us could be there for you. I feel like a right ass that you had to rely on a stranger, albeit a hot one."

"It wasn't what I'd envisaged, that's for sure, but then again, none of this is. I mean look at this." I lift my top to show off my blob of a stomach. "I was *not* expecting this!"

"Is it wrong that I want to touch it?"

"Should I come back later? You two want some alone time?" Kelly marches in, a smirk on her face as she plonks herself down on the bed. "So, what are we touching?"

"This." I lift my shirt again. "It's like I have a giant boob where my stomach used to be."

"Now that's not something you hear every day." She leans over, resting on her elbow as she pokes a finger into the abyss of my belly. "That's just... I don't even know how to describe that."

"Right?"

"I still can't believe he was in there." Sarah stares at my pouch with a look of pure wonder. "It just doesn't seem possible."

Suddenly feeling self-conscious with everyone staring at me, I drop my top back down to cover up. "Well, take my word for it. He was in there." My hand automatically rubs my belly, as it has so many times over the last few months.

"It's so crazy to think you have a kid now. I mean, I can barely get my own shit together, let alone another person's."

"When's he going to wake up?" Sarah whines. "I'm itchin' for a cuddle!" With her hands clutching the side of the crib, she leans in, whispering, "Wake up, James, Aunty Sarah wants to snuggle."

"Shhhhh." That rabbit toy comes in handy once again as I assault her head with it. "Don't wake him!"

"Alright, fine," she huffs, spinning around in her seat to face me again. "Let's get back to Nathan. When're you seeing him again?" She wiggles her eyebrows at me with a cheesy grin.

"Nathan Frost?" Kelly lets out an exasperated sigh. "Really, Jess? Didn't you hear what I said about him?"

"Yes, I did. But you're wrong about him. He's kind and caring, and he was here for me when I needed someone."

"I'll give him credit for that, but I wouldn't be so quick to get on your high horse about him. His brother was down at the station last night, high as a kite. He'd been in some kind of altercation…"

"Let me stop you right there. They are not the same person. Just because Noah is in trouble, doesn't mean Nathan is."

"Not this time. Like I said, he was in an altercation… with his brother."

"That can't be right. He was here with me most of the day," I stammer.

"I'm sorry, Jess. It's true. It must've been just after he left. I heard it was pretty bad." Kelly grabs my hand. "Please, please stay away from him. I don't want to see you get hurt."

"Nathan wouldn't hurt me," I whisper. "He's one of the good ones."

"I'm sure it was some sort of a misunderstanding. Right? You only said Noah was at the station, what about Nathan? Surely if he was in trouble too, he'd be there with him." Always the optimist, Sarah jumps up to wrap her arm around me, offering her support.

"He spent the night in hospital."

"What? He… he got hurt?" My hand flies to my chest as I struggle to take in everything she's saying. "I…I need to see him."

"No. You need to be here for your baby. This is serious, Jess. You need to let it go."

Shaking my head, I push off the bed. "No. You're wrong. I need to see him and make sure he's okay." Turning to Sarah, I ask, "Can you watch James for me?"

# Chapter Seventeen

Nathan

I am officially the worst brother in the world. Noah's going to hate me. *I* hate me. This is an all new low for me. No matter what shit he's gotten into in the past, I have never once ratted him out.

Until now.

If they don't lock him up, they'll probably throw him into some sort of rehab facility. Lord knows he needs it, I'd just hoped he would go of his own volition. I guess that was naïve of me to think. He's an addict, and I've been enabling him. We all have.

Mum likes to pretend that he's this perfect little angel who can do no wrong. She never reprimands him for anything, just blames me instead.

Fuck. She's going to spit tacks when she hears about this – if she hasn't already. I may as well start looking for another place to live now, because there's no way she'll let me stay after this goes down.

I flop back against the puffy pillows, my hands covering my face. *This is a fine mess I've gotten myself into*. Right on cue too. I should have known that as soon as I met someone nice, who likes me for me, the shit would hit the fan. Now I've probably gone and fucked that up too.

Sweet Jess, and baby James. I'd give anything to wind back the clock, never leaving them in the first place. Instead I'm stuck here, nursing a bruised ego and face.

"Nathan?" A strapping woman with sharp features and a brusque tone steps into the room. "You have a visitor. Shall I send them in?"

Assuming it's Officer Delaney back to interrogate me further, I nod, turning my attention back to the garden of green outside the window.

The air in the room changes the instant she steps inside. A small gasp escapes her lips before she says my name. "Nathan? What happened?"

I swallow back the lump in my throat. This is it, the moment when she realises I'm no good for her. When she tells me she doesn't want me coming anywhere near her or James again.

"Why are you here?" I manage to say.

"I… um… I came to see if you were okay. I was worried when you didn't come back yesterday." She doesn't move any closer, just stands by the door, ready for a quick escape.

"Well, here I am." I turn my gaze towards her, and I can see the forgiveness shining through her eyes. I can't let her throw her life away on a worthless piece of shit like me. Steeling my expression, I don't let her see my true feelings. "As you can see, I'm doing just fine." The sarcasm drips from my mouth and I hate myself even more for doing this to her.

"Oh... okay. Um..." Her eyes glisten with unshed tears as she nods towards the door. "Should I... Do you want me to go?" Her voice is barely more than a whisper and I have to fight to keep my hands resting by my side and not wrapping her in my arms.

"It's probably best."

Her face crumples a mere fraction before she controls it. Brushing her hands down the front of her top, she turns and walks to the door. "I'll come and see you before we leave in a day or two."

"Don't bother." *I'm such a fucking asshole.*

# Chapter Eighteen

Jess

With my palm pressed against the wall outside his room, I bow my head, fighting the tears that want to come. My hand finds a place on my still swollen stomach, trying to find some sort of comfort. I will *not* cry. He's hurting and pushing me away, that's all this is.

"You've got to be kidding me!" a harsh, raspy voice says from behind me. "He's gone and knocked some bird up. And you're here for what, sweetheart? A handout?" She belts out a hacking laugh. "Fat chance of that, love. He's not got a cent to his name. Guess you lucked out there."

The smell of stale smoke and alcohol wafts into my face as I stand upright, facing the tiny woman before me. "Excuse me?"

"What'd he promise you? A diamond? A white picket fence?"

"I don't know what you're talking about."

She points at the name on the door, speaking slowly, as if I can't understand English. "You here to see my boy? Nathan? He's gone and got himself into shit again, hasn't he? Not worth the piece of paper his name's written on, that one." I half expect her to spit, she speaks with such spite.

"He's not the father." The words tumble from my mouth before I can stop them. I don't owe this disgusting excuse for a mother any kind of explanation as to why I'm here, but I'm compelled to stick up for Nathan. I have a feeling no one else has. "He's not what you think he is. He's sweet and caring, and he deserves so much more than you give. Why are you even here? To make him feel even worse than he already does?" I fold my arms across my chest, narrowing my eyes.

"How dare you speak to me like that, you little tramp! You think he's such a stand-up guy? Did he tell you he's been to jail? Huh? Or that he was responsible for his father's death?"

"W-what?"

She snorts derisively. "Oh, he left that little piece of info out did he? Yeah, your precious little Nathan killed his own father!" Shoving past me, she barges through the door to his room. I can hear raised voices but no matter how much I try to focus on the words being said, I can't get past the ones spinning around my head. *He killed his father?*

"Jess?" Sarah is on her feet and by my side in a second. "Hun, what's wrong? What's happened?"

"What did he do to you?" Kelly snarls. "I'll kill him."

"No." I shake my head, the irony of her choice of phrasing is not lost on me and for once, I don't want to tell my best friends everything. "I'd like to be alone, if that's okay." The words are barely more than a whisper, but they hear them all the same.

"Oh, okay then. If you're sure?" Sarah draws the corner of her lip into her mouth, watching me intensely.

"Yeah, I'm just really tired." I offer what I hope is a convincing smile, loping over to the bed to sit down.

"Okay, well text if you need anything." Sarah brushes a stray hair behind my ear, her hand resting on my shoulder. "Anytime, okay? I'm here if you need to talk." I nod, patting her hand.

"Thanks. I think I'll try and take a nap while James is sleeping. It was a long night, and I think it's starting to catch up on me now." I curl into the foetal position, dragging my pillow into my arms. Squeezing my eyes shut, I try to block out the altercation with Nathan's mother, but her memory is as persistent as she is. It's no wonder Nathan expected me to run, having that nasty piece of work as a mother. What happened to unconditional love?

*He killed his father.*

The words jump out, reminding me of the horrible things she had said. *You think he's such a stand-up guy... He was responsible for his father's death.* It's those words that give me pause – *responsible for his death*. What does that even mean?

Various scenarios run through my mind, but not one seems like the kind of thing Nathan could be capable of. I refuse to believe that he would willingly end someone's life. Especially his own flesh and blood.

No. There has to be more to this story, and I'll be damned if I don't find out what it is.

# Chapter Nineteen

Nathan

"I bet you're real proud of yourself, huh? Getting your brother in trouble. You know they're going to send him away?" She stands before me with one hand on her hip, the other pointing out the door. Her arm is almost swallowed by the oversized rugby jersey she's wearing over her faded black leggings, and for once, she has her hair tied up off her face. I'm still trying to wrap my head around the fact that she's actually here, in my hospital room and not at the station with Noah. This is the most she's spoken to me in I don't even know how long. "Well? What're you going to do about it?" she demands, folding her arms across her chest, one foot tapping frantically. She hates hospitals. They always remind her of when...

She snaps her fingers in front of my face. "You answer me when I'm talkin' to you."

"Sorry, Ma." I duck my head, an automatic reaction to her raised voice. From an early age I learned it was best to just keep my head down and apologise, no matter whether it was my fault or not. To this day, I still don't know how I managed to hit that cop. I've always been the peacemaker, the one who avoids conflict at all costs. To suddenly land myself in prison, surrounded by men who'd done far worse, was an eye-opener. I saw things no one should ever have to see, and did things no one should ever have to do. All for the sake of saving my brother. And look where that got me. Now he's locked up and I'm out here dealing with the aftermath of his actions, somehow still taking the blame.

I built up a lot of resentment on my time inside. Resentment for the childhood I lost, and for the big brother whose addiction is what put me inside in the first place. I spent many days wondering why he couldn't have been a normal big brother. Why'd he have to be this juvenile delinquent addict who needs constant supervision? And why was it always my job to watch out for him?

"This'll be good for him, you'll see. He's going to get the help he needs."

"Help! He doesn't *need* help!" She begins pacing back and forth. "You're the one that needs help. I mean, look at you." She waves her hand in the air. "You're all kinds of messed up. And don't think I didn't see that bit-on-the-side out there."

My head snaps up at the mention of Jess. I pushed her away for her own good, the last thing she needs is some drop-kick hanging around. "She's not… she's no one."

"Mmm, that why she looked about ready to start ballin'?"

It's like a shot to the heart to hear I made her cry, but it only proves my point. She deserves better than the life I can provide. "Not my problem," I say, schooling my face to a look of boredom, while inside I'm quietly dying.

"Thought as much." She comes up close, poking a finger into my chest, not even caring that I'm black and blue. "You need to fix this shit you've got Noah into. I don't know what you told them, but you need to fix it. Now." She emphasises each word with another poke to the chest.

"Ma, he's an addict, he needs he—" The sharp sting of her hand on my already bruised cheekbone stops me mid-sentence.

"He is *not* an addict. Don't be spreadin' lies about him."

I would never hit a woman, but this is the closest I've ever come to wanting to. "Just because you don't want to see it, doesn't make it any less true." I speak softly, but hold her gaze with an intensity.

"I want you gone. As far as I'm concerned, I only have one son." She turns and stalks to the door, wrenching it open.

An anger wells up inside. An anger I've tried to bury deep down. "You've always only had one. No matter what I do, it's never enough for you. I was a child! I didn't mean for it to happen. When are you going to stop blaming me?"

Her shoulders drop and she stares at something in the hallway as she answers. "You took the love of my life away from me. That's something I can never forget or forgive."

I watch her walk out the door, and out of my life for good. Hot tears fall from my eyes, fogging up my glasses, but I don't care enough to do anything about it. I have nothing and no one, and it's all my fault.

# Chapter Twenty

Jess

The drive back to my parents' place is one of mixed emotions. I've spent the last two days getting to know James and forming some kind of a routine. I've mastered the art of nappy changing, and we've come to an understanding with his feeding times; my milk finally came in, giving him what he needs. Still, I can't help wondering if all this progress will disappear now that we're back in the 'real world'. In the hospital, I had the nurses to help me whenever I needed it, but here, I'll be on my own. Mum and Dad both work, so it's me and James fending for ourselves from now on, and I'm scared. Scared I won't be good at this. Scared I will screw this up somehow. And though I hate to admit it, I'm scared I'll be doing this on my own, forever.

Nathan still won't talk to me. By the time I'd built up the courage to go and see him again, he'd already been discharged. No note, no visit, nothing. He'd just disappeared.

Kelly came by to tell me that Noah had been forced to go to a rehab facility or face charges of wilful damage and grievous bodily harm. I'd deduced that he was the one responsible for Nathan's time in hospital, and it made my blood boil. I'd had a bad feeling about him all along.

James stirs in his capsule beside me, bringing me out of my reverie. I trace soft circles around his chubby cheeks and over his nose, relishing the silky skin under my fingers. "We're home, little man." I wait for the car to come to a stop before unbuckling both of our seatbelts. Taking a deep breath, I open the door, and step out. The house seems smaller somehow. Reaching back into the car, I grab hold of the capsule handle and lift him from the car. "This is your new home," I say, holding him up as if he knows what I'm talking about. "We're gonna stay here for a while, until I can afford to get us a place of our own."

"No rush. We're happy to have you here with us, sweetheart." Dad kisses my forehead before taking the capsule from my hands. "Here, let me grab him for you."

The instant pang in my chest as he is pulled from my arms surprises me. It's as if my body feels that no one but me could possibly look after him.

"It's okay, I've got him." Dad smiles knowingly.

"Twenty-one years and he never dropped you once." Mum came up beside me, draping an arm around my shoulders and pulling me in tight. "Sometimes I think you forget that we've done this all before."

"I know, he's just so little, and fragile…" I let my voice trail off. I'm being silly. Who better to trust with my baby than my parents?

"Come on, let's get you two settled in." She leads me inside, dropping the baby bag by the door. "We've set up a nappy change area in the bedroom for those midnight changes, and I've put a tri-pillow on your bed for feeding."

"Thanks, Mum, you didn't have to do all this."

"Nonsense! This is my first grandchild, let me dote a bit." She smiles, letting go of me and heading straight for James, who is now lying on a blanket on the floor, with my dad lying beside him. She is on all fours, hovering over him in a matter of seconds and I can't help smiling as I watch them.

"Do you mind if I go and have a shower?" I ask, not wanting to interrupt their playing.

"Go right ahead." Mum waves her hand behind her, shooing me away.

I dump my bag on the bed and rummage through my drawers to find something clean to wear. An old pair of trackies and a baggy tee will do; I can't fit much else over the jelly belly that appears to be in no hurry to go anywhere. With a towel in my hand, I traipse through to the bathroom, and turn on the faucet. Stripping out of my clothes, I step under the water and expel a sigh of pleasure. In the few days that I've been away, I'd gotten used to the small hospital shower with only a tiny nozzle and low water pressure. Compared to that, this is like pure heaven. The spray covers my entire body at once, giving me a full body massage, and relieving the tension I didn't know I had.

With each knot unwinding, my mind wanders back to the cause of my concern. *Nathan*. I can't shake the feeling that his mother has him all wrong.

Perching on the edge of my bed, I grab my phone and turn to Google for help. I type Nathan Frost into the search bar and wait. A list pops up with links to the library and his social media account. I scroll down the page until one post jumps out at me. It's an article from the local paper, dated eighteen years ago. Without hesitation, I click on the link.

## Man Killed *in Freak Accident*
October 3rd, 1999

A man was killed outside his home yesterday afternoon, when hit by an oncoming vehicle while saving his son. Mr Roger Frost had been playing in the yard with his two children, Noah and Nathan, when a ball had gone over the fence and onto the road. Mr Frost's three-year-old son had run onto the road to retrieve it, not seeing the vehicles coming towards him. Mr Frost threw his boy to safety in the nick of time, sealing his own fate. He died on impact.

"Oh God, Nathan," I whisper, reading the words over and over as tears fall for the little boy who lost his father that day, and it would seem his mother not long after.

# Chapter Twenty-One

Nathan

Sleeping on Darren's couch isn't all it's cracked up to be. My muscles ache, and it's not just from the lumpy couch that's a foot too small for my whole body to lie on comfortably. It's my own fault really. When I'd shown up unannounced three nights ago, my clothes shoved into plastic bags and nowhere else to go, Darren's mum hadn't been too happy to see me. It'd taken some convincing, but after offering to make amends for Noah's episode by cleaning her house from top to bottom, she begrudgingly accepted.

It'd been demanding work, that's for sure. Darren's dad's hoarding wasn't limited to the back yard alone. No, there was an entire room full of old newspapers and magazines, broken toys from when Darren was a kid, and a whole lot of old kitchen appliances. He'd even started lining the hallway with empty boxes, and I wasn't allowed to move any of them. I don't know how anyone can live surrounded by that much clutter, I felt claustrophobic every time I stepped foot out of the lounge – the only room to be left free of his 'collections'.

Three days is my limit. I need to get out of here. I need to get back to work – if I even have a job to go back to. I know how the gossip mill in this town works. It doesn't take long for stories to spread, and I wouldn't be surprised if over the weekend someone had told my boss a mixed-up version of the truth. In my infinite wisdom, I'd called in sick yesterday, hoping for some sort of miracle cure overnight, but alas, my face is still black and blue with a faint tinge of greenish-yellow around the edges. At least the swelling has gone down.

I pull myself up off the couch, stretching my arms above my head. It's still early, and the house is eerily quiet. I move through to the kitchen to make a coffee, careful not to wake anyone else. Seeing my shoes by the door, I quickly slip them on, edging outside and down the drive to collect the morning paper. The hospital looms in the foreground, and instantly my mind goes back to her; wondering if she's still in there, and how she's doing. I replay our last encounter, seeing the hurt in her eyes when I told her to leave and not come back. What an asshole. I pushed away the one good thing in my life. The one person who believed in me, even when I didn't believe in myself. I just let her walk away.

With a sigh, I bend down to pick up the paper covered in morning dew. My glasses slide down the bridge of my nose, having been loosened during my scuffle with Noah, and I make a mental note to get them fixed during my lunch break as I slowly lope back inside to make my coffee.

Adding the paper to the heap on the table, I move about the kitchen, trying to focus on the day ahead, but I can't stop thinking about Jess, and how I wish things could be different. Perhaps in another lifetime. One where I'm not fighting an uphill battle to prove myself to others. To prove that I'm not the worthless piece of shit they all think I am.

Only, I've gone and proved them all right, haven't I? When shit got hard, I did what I do best, I ran. I hurt someone I really cared about and I ran away. If that doesn't make me worthless, I don't know what does.

I don't deserve to have someone so kind-hearted and beautiful in my life. I'll only end up hurting her even more, and that's something I couldn't live with. She's better off without me. They both are.

Standing outside the library, I straighten my shirt again, and smooth my hand through my hair, hoping like hell they'll let me through the doors. It's not exactly a good look I'm sporting, and I'm half-expecting them to turn me away as soon as they see me.

"Nathan? You coming... Oh my!" Liz, one of the newer librarians gasps, a hand flying to her mouth. "Are you okay? What happened?" She reaches her hand towards me, then pulls back, looking uncomfortable.

I plaster on a smile and force out a chuckle. "You should see the other guy." The words are out before I've thought them through. "Shit, that's not what I meant... I didn't..." Stumbling over my words, I come up blank. What can I say that isn't going to make them scared of me? "I fell?" It comes out as a question, making it clear that I'm lying.

"Oh... well... b-be more careful," she stutters, taking a step away from me. I can see the fear in her eyes and I mentally kick myself for being so stupid.

"Liz..." I reach out, for what I don't know. It doesn't matter anyway; the damage is done. She already thinks I'm bad news.

"I've got to," she hooks her thumb over her shoulder, nodding towards the door. "See ya." She turns and scurries away, probably to tell everyone about the brawler that I am.

With a shake of my head, I push through the doors, prepared for the onslaught.

I keep my head down and make a beeline for the staffroom to drop my bag off. Whispers cease as I walk by, confirming my suspicion. It's only a matter of time before they send me packing.

Avoiding their watchful eyes, I scarper out to the front, grabbing the familiar handles of my trolley. I head to the very back of the library, the squeak of the wheels reverberating around the room, drawing unwanted attention to me. I tuck my head even further into my chest, my glasses once again sliding down my nose, as I pick up the pace.

I can't lose this job. Without it, I have nothing.

"Nathan? A word please." My shoulders slump as I hear the clipped tones of my boss from behind me. For someone so small, she can certainly spread the fear of God into any man with just one word.

I nod my head, turning to follow behind her as she marches back to the office, her practical brown leather loafers making not one ounce of sound. I stare at the back of her short, blonde bob that always seems to be styled to perfection, never moving out of place even at the rapid pace she is currently setting.

Looking at her, it was hard to believe this woman had been a friend of my father's once upon a time. When I'd been locked up, she'd been the only one to come out and see me. She'd taken me in, offering me a chance to redeem myself by working for her. At first I'd thought she was some sort of sexual deviant, trying to lure me in. It wasn't until I'd gone back home that I'd found the box of photos tucked away in the garage. Pictures from when my parents were in high school. They looked so happy back then, carefree and in love. I hadn't seen my mother look like that in a long time, in fact, I struggled to remember a time when she hadn't looked angry at the world.

Tucked in behind one of the framed pictures of their group of friends, was a picture of my father with his arm around a blonde-haired girl. Her hair was longer back then, and her features much softer, but I'd recognised her straight away. Grace Stone. The woman who had offered me a job.

I couldn't bring myself to mention what I'd found to Mum, somehow knowing it would bring her more pain. Instead, I swallowed my pride and walked down to the library to take her up on her offer.

Now, here I sit, in that very same office, waiting for her to let me go. I fold my hands across my lap to stop them from fidgeting, and look around the room, unable to meet her eyes.

"Nathan?" Closing the door, she walks over to her desk, perching on the edge. "Is everything okay?" Her tone has gone from brusque to soothing now that we are away from prying eyes. I forget sometimes that she can be so different behind closed doors.

Letting out a huff of hot air, I lean forward in my seat, my elbows on my knees and my head in my hands. "I don't know what to do."

"You can start by telling me what happened to your face."

# Chapter Twenty-two

Jess

Peeling my eyes open, I swing my legs over the edge of the bed, shoving my feet into my waiting slippers and walk the two steps to the crib where James is squawking.

"Hey there, little man. What are you doing awake again, huh?" I reach in and pull him into my arms, his head bobbing about as he searches for a feed. "Seriously?" I peer at the glowing red numbers of my alarm clock. "It's only been an hour." His snuffling tickles my neck and I suppress a giggle as I carry him over to the change table. "First things first, let's check that nappy."

"Everything okay in here?" Mum stands in the doorway, her dressing gown pulled tight.

"Yeah, Mum. Sorry we woke you."

She waves her hand dismissively. "Don't worry about it. I was going to make a cup of tea, would you like one?"

"That would be nice, thanks." My smile is interrupted by a yawn and I quickly cover my mouth with my spare hand. "Might help me stay awake. This kid seems to be particularly hungry tonight." I place him down on the change mat, slowly unbuttoning his onesie.

"It's probably a growth spurt. They do that every now and again." She slips out and down the hall to the kitchen, leaving me to finish the job at hand.

"All clean and dry," I say, squirting a blob of hand sanitiser onto my hands. By the time I am settled back into bed with James cradled in my arms, his tiny body propped up by a pillow, Mum has placed my tea on the bedside table.

She perches on the edge of the bed. "You know you can always wake me if you need help."

"I know. I can handle it."

"I know you can, but sometimes it's okay to ask for help." Her fingers sweep across my cheek, cupping my face. "I'm really proud of you, you know that?"

"Of me?"

"Yes, you. Not many girls your age would have the courage to walk away from an unhealthy relationship, especially while heavily pregnant. But you? You take it all in your stride. You are going to be a great mum." She brushes a tear away with a chuckle. "Look at me, getting all sentimental in my old age."

"Stop, you're not old." I grab her hand. "Thank you though. That means a lot. Sometimes I have no idea what I'm doing, and I'm so scared I'm going to make the wrong decision. Being a mum is way harder than you made it look."

"You say that like you don't remember the time I forgot to pick you up from netball practice, or the time I let you ride your bike across that field and you fell into the offal pit." She giggles and it makes her seem younger, like the Mum I knew before I got involved with *him*. "Believe me, I was faking it the whole time. No one ever knows what they're doing. You just do the best you can, and hope like hell it all works out." Her eyes lift to mine. "You turned out alright, so I guess I must've done something right."

"Yeah, I guess so." With a sigh, James pulls back, his head flopping back and his mouth hanging open, milk-drunk.

"Here, let me take him for you." Mum holds her hands out, wiggling her fingers as I cover myself up. She props him over her shoulder, rocking back and forth as she pats his back, waiting for a burp. When she's satisfied he's expelled it all, she settles him back in his crib, wrapping him nice and tight. I take a sip of my tea, letting my head fall back against the pillow as I watch them.

"Honey, I want to apologise."

"What for?"

I scoot over, giving her room to join me on the bed. "For the things I said in the hospital."

"You didn't…" She holds her hand up, not letting me finish.

"I did. I shouldn't have said what I did about Nathan. You're right, I don't know him, and I never gave him a chance. I'm sorry if I scared him off."

"Mum, you didn't. It's complicated."

"Well, maybe you should uncomplicate it. I miss seeing that spark in your eye. The one you had when you were younger before all this mess with…" She lets her voice trail off. We have an unspoken rule to never mention his name. "I know you have feelings for Nathan, I could see it in your eyes; that sparkle was back. I don't want you to throw it away because of something I said."

"I tried, Mum. He sent me away. I don't want to be that person again, the one who fights for something that isn't there."

"Honey, it's there. Believe me. What he did for you? That was nothing short of amazing, I was just too stubborn to see it for what it was. He stood by your side and held your hand at what is likely to be one of the hardest moments of your life, and he never left. He was in awe of you, sweetheart, and rightly so."

"You think?" Call it baby blues, or pregnancy hormones, but I cannot stop the tears from falling.

"I don't think, I know." She pats my hand, handing me a tissue. "Now, finish your tea and get some rest before he wakes again. I hate to tell you this, but it's going to be a long night."

# Chapter Twenty-three

Nathan

It's been eight days since I saw her last. Eight days and I still can't get her out of my head. It's like some sort of cruel and unusual punishment my brain is playing on me right now. Like I need any more reminders of how I've fucked up my life.

Those sad blue eyes of hers follow me everywhere I go. No matter how much I try to forget her, I can't. Every perfect detail of her is ingrained in my memory. She's somehow become a part of me without even trying, and I'm stuck wondering if I made the right decision by shutting her out.

I push the creaking trolley through the deserted library aisle, stopping every few shelves to unload the returned books. In the short amount of time I've been working here, I've managed to memorise all the various categories and their coinciding numbers. I can practically do this with my eyes closed, which is both a blessing and a hindrance. It's this autonomy that makes it so easy for my mind to wander back to Jess. I sent her away, I know that, but even so, I keep searching for her amongst the fiction shelves. I find myself staring at the couch where I first talked to her, and imagine a time where it could have worked between us. An alternate universe where I'm not the jailbird with the addict for a brother and an uncaring mother hell-bent on making me pay for something I had no control over. Where Jess had not been hurt by a man who got her pregnant and left her abandoned.

When my eyes refocus and all I'm left with is the threadbare couch and my dreams, I tell myself it's for the best. No point in wishing for an unobtainable fantasy.

Shaking my head to send the visions fleeing, I push the trolley back to the counter to grab the next load. It's monotonous, but it pays the bills, or at least, allows me to give Darren's parents some money. Eight nights on that godforsaken couch. I really need to find a new place to crash. Preferably somewhere with an actual bed. As I run through the short list of friends I could try, I catch a glimpse of blonde hair coming through the doors. It could be anyone, but the hairs on the back of my neck tell me it isn't just anyone.

*Jess.*

She's here. I shouldn't be happy to see her, but damn it I can't help it. I've been miserable these past few days, knowing how much I hurt her. Just another prick to add to the list of let-downs in her life.

"Hey, watch it, buddy!" A jolt runs up my arms as the guy in front of me slams his hand down on the trolley, stopping me in my tracks.

"Sorry, I didn't see you." I apologise, ducking my head, the action an automatic response to anything confrontational.

"Yeah, well, you should be more careful." The guy steps away. "There are kids around here, ya know?" It's then that I see the little girl peering up at me from behind the trolley, her big brown eyes like orbs.

"Shit, I'm so sorry." I rake my fingers through my hair, pulling it to one side. "Let me... um, hang on." I dash around the trolley and up to the counter, heading straight for the box of stickers we keep behind the children's library checkout. With the box in hand, I make my way back over to the little girl and her father. "Would you like to pick a few stickers?" I ask, crouching down to show her.

She looks up at her father. "Can I?" she asks. When he nods, she turns back to the box, poring over the contents. "How many can I choose?"

I look side-to-side before answering. "Well, normally we only give out one at a time, but if you promise to keep it a secret, you can have two." I wink and she giggles, her eyes lighting up.

She chooses one with a pink princess and another with a purple elephant reading a book. "Thank you, Mr. I won't tell nobody." She zips her hand across her lips.

"You're very welcome." I stand up, an apologetic smile on my face. "I really am sorry. I'll be more careful from now on." He nods and I watch them walk out the door hand-in-hand.

"You're really good with kids." Her voice is like one from the heavens, sending my heart racing and drying up my throat. I turn slowly, half expecting to see a mirage.

"Jess," the word falls from my lips on a rasp and I have to blink to make sure she really is standing in front of me.

"Hi," she says softly. Her golden hair frames her angelic face like a halo. She looks radiant, happy. Motherhood suits her. "I... I wasn't sure if you'd be here or not." She waves her arm around the room, looking over her shoulder. "I know I shouldn't have come..."

"No." Once again, the word slips out before I even know what I'm saying. "It's okay, I'm glad to see you. You look good." I shove my hands in my pockets for want of something to do.

"So do you." She looks down at the tiny body strapped to her chest, brushing a kiss to the top of his head, and a pang of jealousy screams through my body.

*Jealous of a baby? That's a new low, even for you.*

"The bruises have gone down." She gestures toward my face, and a part of me wishes she would touch me. "I heard what happened to Noah. I'm sorry." I shrug, but my jaw tenses, giving me away. "I tried to see you again in the hospital but you'd already left. I just needed to know... to see... are you okay, Nathan? Like *really* okay?"

This is the part where I'm supposed to pretend that everything is fine and send her on her way, but I can't bring myself to utter the words. I sigh, my shoulders dropping as I war with myself.

A tentative hand reaches out to brush against mine, sealing our fate. "I'm here if you need someone to talk to."

"I would really like that."

# Chapter Twenty-four

Jess

"Are you sure you don't mind watching him?" I twist my fingers together nervously.

Mum waves her hand dismissively. "Don't be so silly! Of course I don't mind getting to look after my grandson." She crosses the room, tilting my head up to meet her gaze. "Don't ever feel like you can't ask me, okay? You're allowed to have a break."

"It just feels like I'm being a bad mum. I mean, he's only nine days old." My eyes flit back down to the little bundle wrapped up tight in a shawl, sleeping soundly. He'd fallen asleep on the walk home from the library and I hadn't the heart to move him from the pack strapped to my chest. Okay, maybe I was too scared to in case he woke up.

"Listen to me." She unfastens the buckles holding James to my chest, easing him into her arms as she continues to speak. "You are not a bad mum for wanting some time to yourself. This is one of the hardest jobs there is, and you can't be at your best if

you don't have some 'you time' every now and again."
Taking hold of my shoulders, she pushes me towards
the hallway. "Now, go and get ready. He'll be finishing
work soon."

When I'd walked into the library it had been a spur-
of-the-moment decision. It had been the first time I'd
ventured out of the house since leaving the hospital,
and somehow I wound up standing outside the library. I
must've stood there for a good ten minutes before
working up the courage to go inside. I had no idea if
he'd even be there, or if he'd even talk to me, but I had
to at least try.

And now, here I am, staring blankly into my
wardrobe as I realise that I have nothing to wear. I'm
still rocking the jelly-belly and don't really fancy
having that out on display for the world to see. The
only thing close to fitting over my newly formed curves
is a mauve baby-doll dress that ties under the bust. The
skirt billows out enough to flow over my stomach, and
paired with a pair of black leggings it looks passable. I
pull a section of my hair up into a ponytail, leaving a
few tendrils to hang around my face, and then finish
with a dab of lip gloss.

Out in the lounge, Mum has spread a blanket on the
floor, a myriad of toys and books spread around the
outer edges and James lying in the centre. Once again
on all fours, Mum hovers over him, ducking her head
down and back up again in a one-sided game of peek-a-
boo.

"Can I interrupt this game to give him a quick feed before I go?" I drop to my knees, nuzzling my nose into his stomach.

"Probably best." She drags herself up off the floor with an audible oomph. "I'll grab you a cloth so you don't get your outfit all milky." I'm glad one of us is thinking straight.

With James fed and diapered, I kiss his button nose and tell him to behave for Grandma. She holds his tiny hand in hers and makes him wave at me as I walk down the drive and back into town to meet Nathan.

My stomach is tied in knots as I sit in the quaint café down the road from the library, waiting for Nathan to show up. I'd panicked that I wouldn't make it in time and power-walked all the way here, giving me five minutes to rest and calm my nerves. Of course, now that I've stopped moving, my body has gone into overdrive, producing sweat like nobody's business. I keep lifting the hem of my top and billowing it out to allow the cool air to hit my skin. The last thing I want is to be a sweaty mess when he shows up. Not that this is a date or anything. Is it? *Is* it?

Before I can get myself flustered trying to work it out, the door opens and in walks the man with eyes of emerald and gold, the man who is in my thoughts and my dreams. Nathan.

I stand and awkwardly wave so he can see me. When he smiles, I swear my heart just about stops. He's breath-taking. How can so much perfect be wrapped into one body? I can't help but run my eyes up and down his form as he saunters across the room. His dark jeans are fitted, not like those 'home-boys' you see more often than not these days. Anyone who finds baggy jeans that hang around your ass sexy, is just plain crazy if you ask me. Give me a man in fitted jeans any day.

Continuing my appraisal of him, I take in his buttoned-up shirt with the sleeves rolled up, exposing his tanned muscular forearms. An image of those arms wrapped around me pops into my head and I suddenly feel flustered. My fingers begin to play with the hem of my top as I avert my gaze.

"Wow, Jess, you look… beautiful." I've heard those words before, but this is the first time I've truly believed them.

"Thank you," I say in a breathy voice, brushing my hair behind my ear. What is it about him that makes me turn into this soft girly-girl?

He pulls a seat out and sits down, his hands clasped on the table in front of him. He coughs a few times, clearing his throat before grabbing the pitcher of water on the table and pouring some into a glass. Holding it out to me, he asks, "You want some?"

I hold my glass out while he pours, both of us sitting in awkward silence.

"How's James doing?" he finally asks, one thumb gently tapping on the other.

"He's really good. Putting on heaps of weight. He's changed so much and it's only been nine days." I shake my head, still coming to grips with these facts myself.

"Really? It's crazy how quickly things can change." He speaks quietly, and I wonder if we're still talking about James.

"Uh… How's Noah doing? Have you seen him?"

He shakes his head. "Nope. No family allowed."

"Oh, is that… is that normal?" I ask, unsure of the correct protocol.

His shoulders lift in a small shrug. "I have no idea. This is the first time." I place my hand on top of his, my thumb linking with his. "All these years I've been covering for him, and I never realised that I was the one enabling him. I should've been the one stopping him."

"Nathan, you don't control him. He made his choices, just like you did. You can't keep taking the blame for his actions. Unless you physically held him down and injected the needle yourself, this isn't your fault."

"I may not have pulled the plunger, but I provided the cash. I covered for him whenever he got in trouble. I may as well have been the one holding the needle." He paused, his eyes following the movement of our hands together. "I dobbed him in, Jess. I'm the one who put the final nail in the coffin. I outted my own brother."

"Hey." I stroked my thumb along the side of his hand until he looked up at me. "You did what you had to do. He needed the help, and you know it. What you did was brave."

"Brave?" he scoffed. "I threw him under the bus."

"Was he the one who did a number on your face?"

"Yeah, but…"

"No but about it, Nathan. He attacked you. Your own brother attacked you and left you all battered and bruised. What if you hadn't been there? What if it had been someone else? *He* did this to himself." The conflict in his eyes made my chest ache for him. "You need to let go of the guilt. This isn't your cross to bear."

"You guys ready to order?" A waitress appeared beside us, oblivious to the intensity of our conversation.

Nathan turns his head from her view, so I order us both a cappuccino to go.

"Let's get out of here. I think we could use some fresh air, don't you?"

# Chapter Twenty-five

Nathan

Strolling through town with Jess by my side is nothing short of amazing. This girl is like no one I've ever met before. She doesn't see the loser that everyone else does, and somehow, she makes *me* believe I'm not that guy either. I almost feel like maybe it wouldn't be so bad for us to be together. Like maybe I wouldn't be a complete screw up if I had her there to balance me.

I'm getting ahead of myself though. I'm not foolish enough to think this is a date or anything. God, I wish it was though. I'd give anything to have her by my side for as long as she'd have me. Just to be able to hold her, and make her smile, that would really be something. Dreams are free, I guess.

"So, I met your mum… at the hospital," she says, peering up at me through her lashes. "She's um… interesting."

"Interesting? That's one way of putting it I guess." I grab her takeaway cup from her hand and throw it in the trash on the way past. "I hope she wasn't too rude to you."

"Well…"

"Shit, she was, wasn't she? Fuck, I'm sorry, Jess." I take her hand, pulling her to face me. "She's an alcoholic," I say as if it's any kind of excuse for her behaviour. "We don't really get on… I didn't even expect to see her to be honest. I should've known it was only to have another go at me. She kicked me out."

"Wow. She kicked you out? Really? I mean, she did seem pretty angry, but, I never expected…" Shaking her head, she looked up at me with a strange expression on her face. "She thought, um…" I watch as she places her hand on her stomach, and I brace myself for what she's about to say. "She thought you 'knocked me up'—her words."

"Ah shit, I'm so sorry."

"You don't have to apologise, you didn't make her say it." She reaches her hand up to my cheek, her thumb brushing the corner of my mouth. "You take on everyone's issues, don't you? You shoulder the blame for so much, and they have no right to expect that of you." Her voice breaks and I search her eyes for signs of tears. "Nathan, I have to tell you something."

*Shit. Here it comes. The "We can't see each other again" speech.* I swallow the lump in my throat. "Okay, what is it? Is everything okay?" I find myself mirroring her position, cupping her face in my own hands as if I can somehow stop her from saying the words.

"She told me something that I'll admit, scared me at first." *Oh shit.* "But I did a little research on you." She lowers her eyes and a pink tinge colours her cheeks. "I know what happened to your dad."

"Um…"

"I'm sorry, I know I should've just asked you, but I didn't know if you were going to talk to me again."

"Jess, it's okay." I sigh, dropping my hand to my side. "I would've told you eventually. It-It's not really an easy thing to slip into conversation."

"She blames you, doesn't she? You were the one he ran out after?"

I nod, turning away from her piercing gaze. If she keeps looking at me that way, I feel like I will cry and I don't want her to see that again.

When she slips her hands around my waist and presses her head against my chest, I very nearly fall apart. It takes everything in me to keep from balling like a baby. Instead, I tentatively place my arms around her, pulling her in to me. Her soft body provides so much comfort and I'm afraid to let her go. This is what I imagine love feels like – a warm embrace with no hidden agendas.

"It's not your fault, Nathan. None of it." The words are muffled against my chest, but I hear them loud and clear. "It's not your fault."

"It's just up here, the one with the little wooden fence." Jess points down the road and I follow with my eyes. Of course she'd live in the house with the little picket fence. It suits her perfectly. "I'm staying with Mum and Dad until I can save enough to move into my own place."

"That sounds like a smart thing to do. I'm kind of between places too."

"You don't have a place to stay?" Every time she turns those big blue eyes on me, I am hit with a need to make her happy.

"I'm okay." I shrug. "I've been staying with a friend. I'll find a place soon, don't worry." She purses her lips and I want nothing more than to smooth them out with my fingertip. To feel how soft they are beneath mine.

We stop just outside her house and I'm suddenly hit with nerves. I want so much to kiss her, but I don't want to overstep that boundary. We've spent the last half hour with our fingers entwined, our bodies pressed up against each other.

*God, what's wrong with me? I don't get nervous around girls.*

She looks up at me expectantly, the hint of a smile on her face. "I had a really nice time tonight." She swings our hands between us playfully.

"Really? Even with all the depressing shit?"

"Even with all the depressing shit." She nods with a grin.

"Thank you for, well, everything. I had no idea where to find you and I didn't really think you'd want anything to do with me after…"

Her fingers land on my lips. "Stop. You were there for me when I needed you, and I'm going to be there for you too. For as long as you'll let me."

"You better get comfortable then, because I don't think I can let you go."

"Really?" she says softly, surprise all over her face.

"Really." I bring my hand up to her face, tilting her chin upwards. "I've never met anyone like you before, Jess. You see the good in me, but I don't think you see how amazing *you* are."

"I'm not anything special."

"See? You are so much more than special. I wish you could see yourself through my eyes." I dip my head closer to hers, my eyes finding her lips. "You are everything," I whisper, brushing my lips against hers. They're even softer than I'd imagined them to be. With a sigh, I pull away, pressing my forehead to hers. "When can I see you again?"

# Chapter Twenty-six

Jess

"Looks like you had an enjoyable time," Mum says with a knowing smile. "You gonna see him again?"

I can't wipe the goofy grin off my face, and my fingers keep brushing my lips where his had been only moments ago. "Yeah, it was nice. I really like him, Mum. I can't explain it, there's just something about him."

"That's exactly what I felt about your father when we first met." A wistful smile plays across her face as she looks at Dad.

"We're just happy to see you smile like that again. It's been missing for quite some time." He hands Mum a cup of coffee, placing one on the table for himself. "You want one?" he asks.

"Sure, I'll make it, you sit down." I remove my jacket and hang it on the hook by the door before helping myself to a cup. "How was James? Did he behave?"

"He was a dream. Barely a peep from him all night."

"Thanks again for watching him for me. It was nice to get out of the house for a while."

"Like I said, anytime. We're happy to help." Mum grabs the remote and begins searching the guide. "We were just about to watch a movie if you want to join us."

"Thanks, but I think I might call it a night. I got a new book to read when I was at the library earlier, and I'd like to make a start on it." Grabbing my coffee, I give them both a kiss goodnight before leaving them to their movie.

James is sleeping peacefully in his crib, his tiny lips making small suckling movements. It makes me wonder if he's dreaming about feeding.

Stripping out of my clothes and into one of my oversized tees, I slide into bed, pulling the blankets up around me. Adjusting the lamp so that the light doesn't shine on James, I grab my book and open to the first page.

Beside me, my phone vibrates with an incoming message.

**Thank you for taking a chance on me. Sweet dreams, Nathan xxx**

Even in text he's appealing. My fingers automatically trail along my lips once more, my mind taking me back to the moment his lips touched mine, and a slow smile spreads across my face. He has no idea what he does to me.

With quick fingers, I type out a response.

**You call it taking a chance, I call it following my heart. You make mine sing without even trying. Jess xxx**

I push send before I can chicken out and delete it. My heart is in my throat as I watch to see if he responds. A minute goes by and my phone screen switches to 'lock'. *I said too much. I scared him off.*

Placing my phone back on the bedside cabinet, I pick up my book and attempt to read again, but my mind keeps wandering back to Nathan. God, I wish there was an 'undo' button on phones. I never should have said that. It's too much too soon.

When my phone vibrates again, I just about jump out of my skin.

**I wanted to come up with something poetic to say back to you, but it's not really my strength. Here goes:**

**Just a glimpse of your smile,**
**Excites me to no end.**
**So lucky that I found you,**
**Sweet angel, take my hand.**

**I know, it's corny ☺**

I read it over and over, my smile growing bigger each time.

**It's not corny. I love it, thank you xxx**

My phone has barely left my hand when it buzzes again.

**I meant every word. Sweet dreams, Angel. I'll see you tomorrow.**

Too distracted to focus on my book, I put it back where I found it and switch the light off. Snuggling down into my blankets with a happy grin, I let my mind drift. The last thing I see before I fall asleep, are eyes of emerald green.

The children's library is packed with mothers and their babies or toddlers, eagerly awaiting story time. I know James is too young to really understand what is going on, but it's something to do away from the house, and a way for me to meet some other mums. Not to mention the eye-candy lingering in my peripheral. Nathan is meant to be shelving books in the other section of the library, but he seems to keep finding reasons to stop by. It's cute really.

It's amazing the difference in him from yesterday to today. I almost had to do a double take when I saw him beaming at me bright and early this morning. He was ready and waiting at the end of our drive, with two takeaway coffees in hand. He had gone out of his way so that he could walk us to the library in time. He'd helped me with my bag, and even took over pushing the pram for me so that I could savour my drink. He is such a sweetheart. It amazes me that no one has snatched him up already.

A tall, slender woman approaches the group, her kind smile lighting up her face. She's wearing a long, floral skirt that flows around her ankles, and her ebony hair has flecks of grey showing through. When she takes a seat in front of the group, a hush falls over the room, and she begins to read.

It's quite relaxing sitting on a bunch of cushions, being read to. Her lilting voice carries so much expression and cadence that it's almost hypnotic. The children sit, mesmerised by her, the adults relieved to have some peace and quiet. Even some of the librarians have joined the group, dotted around the room, leaning on shelves as they listen.

I catch Nathan's eye as he carries an armload of books to a nearby shelf. He seems so much more relaxed today, more at ease with himself. The burdens he'd been carrying around on his shoulders, no longer weighing him down. This is the Nathan I first met and fell for.

With the story coming to an end, everyone begins to amble out the door, the room empties faster than it had filled. I pop James back into the pram, making sure his hat is pulled down over his ears. We make a quick detour around the fiction section, my eyes scanning the shelves for anything new and exciting.

I feel him before I see him. My skin pricks up, already attuned to his presence, as he comes up behind me. "Can I see you tonight?" he whispers in my ear, sending a shiver through my body. I want so much to say yes, but it doesn't feel right asking my parents to babysit two nights in a row. "Even if it's just a walk after dinner. We can take James with us," he says as he carries on shelving books behind me. It's as though he can read my mind.

Without turning around, I answer breathily, "Sure. I'd like that." The confident Nathan who I met last week is back, and I like it.

"Great, I'll come by around seven. Until then, Angel." He turns back toward his trolley, his fingers brushing lightly against my arm as he passes. When he gets to the end of the aisle, he winks and then walks away as if he has not a care in the world.

# Chapter Twenty-seven

Nathan

I still can't believe she's mine. I've had to pinch myself every day since she came into the library two weeks ago. We've spent every evening together, getting to know each other, and the more I know about her, the deeper I fall for her. She is the most amazing person I've ever met. Her ex was a fool for letting her go, but even though he caused her pain, I'm grateful for it, because now I get to be the one to make her smile, and hear her laugh.

Which she is doing right now, as she lies on the floor, making silly animal noises at James.

"Watch this," she says gleefully. She purses her lips and a long, deep "moo" comes from her mouth, making James startle. She giggles and trails her finger along one of his cheeks. "The cow goes moooooo," she says again, softer. It never fails to amaze me how natural she is at this whole motherhood gig. She seems to take everything in her stride, never faltering.

Without even trying to, she's shown me what a family is meant to look like. How it's meant to feel. I was three when my father died, and not one of my memories feels the way Jess makes me feel. She truly is an angel sent from heaven.

Which is why I wanted to do something special for her. "Hey, seeing as it's so nice out, do you wanna go for a walk?" My voice falters in the middle, but she doesn't seem to notice.

"Sure, just let me get a bag ready." She jumps up from the floor. "Will you watch him for me?"

"Of course, you don't even have to ask." I wiggle closer to the tiny bundle on the floor, holding a finger out for him to grasp. "Hey, little fella," I say softly. "You wanna go for a ride? Yeah? Let's go and get your pram, shall we?" I scoop him up in my arms and carry him over to the pram sitting behind the couch, always up and ready. I pull the covers back and place him down on the soft cushion, strapping him in before covering him back up with the blanket. I fish around underneath the seat to find a hat for him. "Here we go." Pulling the black hat with a silver fern in the centre over his head, I release the brake and manoeuvre the pram out of its resting place.

By the time we have got down the steps outside, Jess is back with her purse and a nappy bag. She throws them into the basket under the seat and takes my hand.

"Where to?" she asks, taking a deep breath of the fresh air outside.

"There's something I want to show you. It's just around the corner."

"Ooh, sounds interesting. Is that my only clue?"

"Yip, that's all you're getting from me. Of course, I'm open to persuasion," I say, puckering my lips and wiggling my eyebrows. She laughs, but grabs my shirt and pulls me down to meet her lips all the same. I run my tongue along her bottom lip, and she opens her mouth a fraction, allowing me access. With one hand cupping her face, I step in closer, needing to feel her against me. She hums against my lips, curling her hand behind my neck and through my hair. I run my hand down to the small of her back, giving a gentle nudge before breaking away with a sigh. "You're not making this easy, you know?" I have to adjust myself so that we can walk without me getting arrested for indecent exposure.

She giggles, her cheeks reddening in that gorgeous way that makes her eyes sparkle. "Sorry. It's only another four weeks, the midwife said. Then, I promise I'll make it up to you."

Grabbing her hand and pulling it to my lips, I plant a kiss on her palm. "You know I'm only joking. I'll wait as long as you need."

"Thank you," she says, her smile lighting up her face. "Now, what did you have to show me?"

Now that it has come down to it, I'm a little nervous about how she'll react to my surprise. When the opportunity had come up, it'd seemed like such a good idea, but now I'm worried that it was a little presumptuous on my part. We've only been seeing each other for a few weeks for God's sake. What the hell was I thinking?

"Stop stressing, I'm sure whatever it is will be amazing." She gives my hand a squeeze and begins to swing it between us. Her smile is infectious, and even though I'm nervous as hell, I find myself grinning back at her.

"I really hope you think so. I swear, I'm not trying to be a creep."

"Well now I'm even more intrigued. How much further?" She cranes her neck past me, searching for whatever it could be. I'm quietly confident she'll never guess it though. Only a fool would be so stupid as to do something like this on a whim.

Pulling the pram to a stop, I wave my hand to my side sheepishly. "Surprise."

Jess looks behind me, her eyes narrowed and lips pursed. She cocks her head to the side and puts one hand on her hip. "I don't get it. What am I looking at exactly?"

"Um," I rub the back of my neck, peering up at her. "Your new place?" *Oh, you're asking her now? Smooth.*

"Yeah, right. Really, I'm not getting it." She looks at me, confused. My shoulder lifts in a shrug as I stare back, and I watch her expression change from confusion to realisation. "You're serious?"

"Um, yeah?" *Goddamn it! Again with the question.* "I um, know you were wanting to find a place for you and James, and when I saw this place was up for rent I put down a bond to secure it for you. I hope that's okay."

"I... are you for real?" She begins to look behind her, as if she's expecting someone to jump out with a camera and yell *"Surprise! You've been punked!"*

"Yeah. Shit, I should've checked with you first, I knew I should've checked with you first, I just thought maybe it would be a cool surprise, and now I can see that it was stupid and—"

"Nathan, stop!" She clamps her hand over my mouth, giggling. "Have I ever told you how cute you are when you're nervous?"

"Um, no," I answer, my lips brushing against the inside of her hand.

Her eyes glisten as she peers up at me and I can't read her expression. "You really did this for me?"

With her hand still across my mouth, I nod. "Is that okay?"

"I think this is the sweetest thing anyone has ever done for me." She lets her hand slide down to my shoulder as she leans in, close enough that I can feel her breath on my lips. "Thank you."

# Chapter Twenty-eight

Jess

"He bought you a house?" Sarah squealed, the magazine in her hand falling to the floor. "Are you kidding me?"

"He didn't *buy* me a house, he just set up a rental for me. Paid the bond and put it in my name. We can move in a few weeks."

"And by we you mean?" Kelly leaned her hip against the counter, blowing across the top of her cup to cool it down.

"Me and James."

"And he's not expecting to move in with you?" She raised her brow sceptically.

"Seriously? We've been together a few weeks now, can you please just try and give him a chance? For me?" I fold my arms across my chest. I know she means well, but the *'he's not good enough for you'* routine is getting a little redundant.

A sigh escapes her lips as she places her coffee on the counter. "I'm sorry, I'm trying. I am, it's just, doesn't it seem a little odd that he'd get you a place when he hasn't got a place for himself yet?"

"I think it's romantic," Sarah pipes up from her perch on the couch. "He wants to look after you."

"Or, he wants to *seem* that way, while secretly hoping you'll invite him to move in."

"Would that be so wrong?" I ask, turning my attention to James who is playing on the floor.

"Oh my God, you've already asked him to, haven't you?" The look of incredulity on her face irks me and I don't know if it's because she knows me better than I thought, or because deep down I know she's probably right.

"No, I haven't. Not yet, anyway." I glance up at Sarah, knowing she'll have my back. True to form, she grins and claps her hands.

"It's so perfect!"

Kelly moves over to me, placing her hands on my shoulders and tilting her head until I look at her. "Jess, you know I'm just trying to look out for you. Please, just think this through, okay? Don't rush it."

"I know. I won't, don't worry."

She pulls me in for a hug, and with a shake of her head, she says, "I swear, you two will be the death of me. One of us has to be the level-headed one." She grins, but I know there's some truth to her words. Over the years, Kelly has taken on being our voice of reason. She has an in-built 'shit-detector' that neither Sarah nor I seem to be blessed with. I've lost count of the amount of times she has kept us from biting off more than we can chew, and I'm grateful for every last one of them. I just hope that this time, she's wrong.

"Are you sure about this? You know we don't mind having you and James here with us." Mum sits on the edge of my bed, watching me pack knick-knacks into boxes.

"I know you don't, Mum. But I feel like we need to do this. It was only meant to be temporary."

"By temporary I thought you meant six months, maybe a year, not a few weeks. Are you sure you're ready to be on your own with a new baby?"

My hands drop to my side. "You don't think I can do it?"

"That's not what I said and you know it. It's tough being a parent, and even harder when you're both Mum and Dad." She reaches out, grabbing the framed picture of me holding James in the hospital, her fingers brushing over the image. "I just don't want you feeling like you need to rush out. We like having you here. Both of you." She hands me the picture and it's then I see the glint in her eye.

"Oh, Mum, we're going to miss you too." I quickly move to stand in front of her, wrapping my arms around her and squeezing. "We'll be right around the corner. You can visit any time you want."

"I know. It's just not the same as having you here with us. I've gotten kind of used to you being home again." She pulls back, fanning her face with her hands. "You wait. When your kids are grown and have moved out, you'll be a blubbering mess like me too." She smiles through her tears. "You'll always be my baby. The worry never goes away, it simply changes form."

With a smile, I hand her a tissue. "I can only hope that I'll be as good at this whole mum thing as you were, and still are."

"Oh stop, you'll make me start again." She pushes off the bed, grabbing one of the flattened boxes by the door. "Right, what's next to pack then?"

# Chapter Twenty-nine

Nathan

"What do you mean he got out?" I pace the length of Darren's lounge, my hands clasped behind my neck. "90 days, that's how long they told me it'd be. How the hell can he be out in less than twenty?"

"I don't know, man. All I know is, he ain't there no more." He stood with his back to the wall, one leg bent at the knee. "Can you stop, with the pacing? You're making me nervous."

"Good! We should be!" I throw my arms up in exasperation. "You know he's going to be looking for me, right? There's no way they let him out willingly. Twenty days doesn't even begin to scratch the surface of addiction, and he'll be looking for the person who got him locked away. Me." I rake my hands through my hair, dropping to a squat in the middle of the floor. "Shit, man, he's gonna be livid. I can't stay here, it'll be one of the first places he'll look."

"Where will you go?"

"I don't know, but I'll figure it out. It's probably better if you don't know anyway. Easier if you don't have to lie for me."

"I may be Noah's friend, but I've still got your back. I'm no snitch, you know that, bro." He pushes off from the wall, offering me a hand, which I accept.

"Thanks for letting me know, and for letting me crash here for so long. I really appreciate it." Turning to the couch I've called home for the last few weeks, I gather my things into a bag.

"Hey," he slaps his hand down on my shoulder. "You know you've always got a place here. I know Mum put up a fight, but deep down, she's grateful that you showed up when you did. No one else was game enough to step in and talk him down."

I lift my shoulder in a shrug. "I just did what any brother would do." With a sigh, I take a seat on the couch. "I've never seen him like that before. It was fuckin' scary, man."

"I know. Fuck, how did it get this bad? I don't remember a time when he wasn't on something." He shakes his head. "I hate it, man. We've been friends since kindy, and I'm watching him waste his life away on this shit. At least you did something about it. What did I do? Jack shit, that's what."

"Fat lot of good it did me though, right? Kicked out of home, disowned."

"That shit is messed up and you know it. She'll come around." I stare at him with my brow raised. "You're right, she won't."

"Not a chance in hell." Grabbing hold of my bag, I jump to my feet. "I'd better get outta here. Maybe I'll see ya round?" I hold my hand out, waiting for Darren to slap it in our customary 'bro-shake', but he pulls me in for a hug instead, thumping my back with his fist.

"Take care, man."

Stepping outside with my bag thrown over my shoulder, I wonder where the hell I'm going to go now. I have no idea how long he's been out, or if he's even in town yet, but I can't hang around here and wait. Pulling my phone from my pocket, I scroll through the names as I walk. Where can I go that Noah won't find me?

*Jess.* The word is a whisper inside my head. *He wouldn't know where to find me there…* As tempting as that is, I can't allow her to be dragged into this mess. She's too pure, too innocent. I never wanted her to be a part of this fucked up world I live in, which is exactly why I should've stayed away from her. I can't let him ruin her too.

"Shit," I hiss, staring at her number on my phone. The decent thing to do would be to leave, get out of her life before she gets sucked in to the black hole that is my life. Punching out a quick message, I hit send before I can change my mind.

**Jess, you are everything I never knew I wanted. I wish I could give you the world. Please don't try to find me. I need you to be safe.**

**Forever in my heart, Nathan xxx**

My heart jumps into my throat the second I push the button, but there's no going back now. She's going to hate me, and I wouldn't blame her. *I* hate me. Why the fuck did I think life would let me have her? Everyone I love eventually leaves, I'm just getting in first this time.

My phone pings within seconds.

**Nathan, you're scaring me. What's going on? Maybe I can help. Please talk to me.**

It takes all my restraint to stop myself from responding. Instead, I find Sarah's number.

**Jess needs you. Tell her I'm sorry. I never meant for any of this to happen.**

Walking the streets, I continue to scroll through my phone until I find the only person I can think of who can help me. With a heavy heart, I dial.

"Hey, it's me. Um, can I stay with you please?"

# Chapter Thirty

Jess

"Sweetie? You okay?" Sarah pushes my bedroom door open, and the look on her face tells me she knows already. "Your mum said you were in here." She tip-toes over to the bed and sits down by my feet.

"How did you know I needed you?" I ask as silent tears fall down my face.

"Nathan text me." She holds her phone out to show me the message. "What happened?"

I shrug. "I have no idea. I was sitting here feeding James when I got this message from him." I grab my phone and read it out. "Jess, you are everything I never knew I wanted. I wish I could give you the world. Please don't try to find me. I need you to be safe. Forever in my heart, Nathan, kiss, kiss, kiss." I drop the phone into my lap. "What does that even mean?" James stirs in his crib so I lower my voice. "Please don't try to find me, I need you to be safe? Is someone coming after him? After us?" My voice falters and I drop my head into my hands.

Sarah's cool hand rests on my leg. "Does your mum know?"

I shake my head. "No. What would I even say? *I* don't even know what's going on." Grabbing a tissue from my bedside table, I swipe the tears from my face. "Why won't he talk to me? We could work something out together. He shouldn't be dealing with whatever it is on his own."

"Did you try calling him?"

"He turned his phone off."

"Maybe you could send him a message, let him know that you're here for him. It might be what he needs to hear. You said yourself, he's never had anyone on his side before. Maybe he's not used to relying on others." Her words make sense. His own mother turned her back on him. "Send him one a day, make him see that you're not going anywhere."

"Okay, that makes sense." I grab my phone and type out a message.

**If you're in trouble, I'm here for you. No matter what it is, you can talk to me.**

**Forever and Always, Jess xxx**

"Done." I let the phone fall beside me on the bed. "Can we keep this between us for now? I don't know if I can deal with Kelly's '*I told you so*' speech right now."

"Of course." She zips her lips closed with her fingers. "My lips are sealed."

"Thanks." My eyes land on the boxes lined by the door. "Oh shit."

"What?"

"What am I meant to do about the house now?" I wave my hands towards the boxes.

"What do you mean? It's in your name, isn't it?"

"Yeah, but it seems wrong to be moving there when he's not returning my calls, don't you think?"

"You've still got over a week until moving day. Give him some time, I'm sure he'll come around by then." She wraps her arms around me, pulling me in for a hug. "Don't stress, it'll all sort itself out."

"I hope you're right."

"I always am," she says in a sing-songy voice before kissing the top of my head. "Come on, let's leave this little guy to sleep." She drags me from my room and down the hall to the bathroom. Pushing me in, she says, "Go wash your face and comb your hair so you look respectable. I'm taking you out for some fresh air."

"No, I can't… James…" I start.

Sarah holds her hand up to stop me. "Jess, let me handle it." With her hands on her hips, I know I have no choice but to follow her instructions. For someone so sweet, she can be very pushy when she wants to be.

When I'm done freshening up, she again takes me by the shoulders and leads me out to the lounge.

"Hey, Mrs Ferguson, do you mind if I borrow Jess for a bit?" She puts on a harrowed expression. "I could really use a friend right now, and Jess is good to talk to."

"Yeah, of course. I hope everything's okay?"

Sarah waves her hand in front of her. "Yeah, it will be. I've just got a lot on my mind. Boy stuff, ya know?"

"Isn't it always?" Mum says with a smile. "Don't let them walk all over you, Sarah. You've a heart of gold, don't let it get tarnished." She rests her hip on the corner of the bench, turning to me. "When's he due for a feed?"

I check my watch before answering. "Not for another hour. I should be back by then, though." I look at Sarah for confirmation and she nods.

"Oh yeah, it won't take long. I just think better in the fresh air." She hooks her arm through mine, leading me across the room and out the door.

"Thanks, Mum!" I call out before the door closes. "Okay, who are you and what did you do with my friend?" I ask, squinting at the girl beside me. "You just lied to my mum. You *never* lie."

"You didn't want her to know, so I covered for you." She shrugs as if it's no big deal. "You're welcome."

"Well, thank you." We walk in silence to the end of the block. "Where are we going?"

"You're going to show me your new pad, silly."

"I don't know…"

She stops, turning to face me. "Jess, he got the place for you. Stop being so stubborn. This is the closest thing to a fairy tale I'm ever going to get, so humour me."

"What part of this is like a fairy tale? The part where he disappears?"

"You're exasperating sometimes, you know that?" She shakes her head, her eyes rolling. "Let me break it down for you. He came to your rescue when you were in labour," she counts on her fingers as she continues to talk, "He provided you with your very own kingdom, and of course, like all fairy-tale princes, he wants to protect you and keep you from harm. Ooh, and he has the evil mum, who in turn, becomes your wicked stepmother!" She claps her hands like a child who's just discovered dessert.

"I don't think that's how it works…"

"Shhh, potatoes, potahtoes." She flicks her hand in the air. "Mark my words, he will come back for you, they always do. You will get your happily ever after."

One of the many reasons I love Sarah so much, is her infinite optimism. It's almost impossible to deny her when she goes off on one of her crazy tangents and even if you could, you wouldn't want to because she makes it sound so magical. As they always do, the tingles start in my stomach and spread through my body as I let myself believe that maybe this time, she could be right.

# Chapter Thirty-one

Nathan

Three days of not seeing Jess and I feel as though I'm losing my mind. I've gotten so used to her being a part of my life that everything feels wrong without her. I can't even use my work as a distraction because that's the first place Noah would look. Thanks to Darren, I know he's already done the rounds of our usual haunts. I can't hide from him forever though. Maybe I should just go home and get it over with. Face the music, so to speak.

The ping of my phone grabs my attention and I quickly snatch it up, knowing it'll be a message from Jess. She's sent me one, sometimes two, a day since I walked out. Each time she tells me she's there for me, and that she cares. It's become the highlight of my day.

Sitting in Grace's sleepout, staring at blank walls for hours on end doesn't exactly give me much to look forward to, and even though I know I should be letting her go, I can't stop the hope from blossoming every time I get one of those messages.

This time is no different.

**Nathan, I miss you. I hope you're okay, wherever you are. Please come back to me. I'm not giving up on you. On us either.**

**Forever and Always, Jess xxx**

God, I miss her too. I find myself scrolling through the pictures on my phone, just so I can get a glimpse of her smiling face. She has this inner strength that I can only wish for. I don't know how she does it, but it's as if nothing gets to her, nothing flusters her. And yet, I still find the need to protect her and keep her safe. I don't know what I'd do if anything were to happen to her or James because of me.

"Another message?" Grace asks, stepping through the open door with a plate in her hand.

"Yeah, she says she's not going to give up on me."

She purses her lips, holding the plate in the air. "I brought you something to eat. I've got to head back into work soon, but, Nathan? Why don't you call her? I can see that you want to." She places the plate beside me then steps back. "Whatever this thing is between you and Noah, it's not going to go away. You're going to have to face him some time. And Jess *obviously* cares about you. Don't let her get away."

"I was actually thinking the same thing. I think I'll go and see Noah tonight."

"And Jess?" she prompts.

"I don't know…"

"I know this isn't my business, but," she kneels on the floor, her hand reaching for mine, "don't you think it's time for you to get what you want for a change?"

When I look up at her, she continues. "You have spent your life trying to make everyone else happy. When do you get your time?"

"Maybe I don't get my turn. Maybe this is my punishment for Dad."

She reaches up, grasping my face in her hand. "Stop it. I'm not your mother, and I will not sit here and listen to you talk about giving up. What happened to your father was an accident. It was no one's fault. You have shouldered the blame for this for far too long." She stands up, brushing the dust from her knees. "I have to get to work, but if you like, I can come with you tonight. You shouldn't have to face them alone, and to be honest, I'd quite like the chance to tell your mother to pull her head out of her ass and see the brilliant kid she's got right in front of her." She huffs, folding her arms across her chest. "What do you say?"

"You'd really do that for me?" I ask, taken aback by the intensity of her words.

"Of course I would. It's something I should've done a long time ago. Your father would hate to see you living like this."

"You never did tell me what happened between you two."

Her eyes soften and she stares off wistfully. "We were very close, your father and I. High school sweethearts even, for a time. My parents were very strict though, and once they found out, they forbid me from seeing him anymore. They sent me to an all-girls school for a year, and by the time I was allowed to go back, he'd already met your mother." She turns her gaze on me. "They were very much in love. I never stood a chance."

"I'm sorry."

"Don't be. All I wanted was for him to be happy, and he was. I could see it in his eyes. She was the light of his life." She steps out the door, looking back over her shoulder. "I've got to go back in now, but I'll see you at five. We can head over then."

I nod. "Okay, if you're sure you don't mind?"

"I wouldn't offer if I didn't want to do it. You're a good kid, Nathan. You don't deserve to be treated like shit."

"Thank you." I'm not sure it was entirely the right response, but it's all I could think to say. What are the odds? A lifetime spent thinking I wasn't good enough, and in the space of a few months, I meet two incredible women who see through all the bullshit. They see me. And damn it feels good.

The ride over to Mum's has my stomach in knots. I haven't spoken to her since that day in hospital, and I really have no idea what I'm going to say when I get there.

Grace tried to make conversation, but in the end, we settled on silence. It still amazes me that even after only knowing me a brief time, she is still willing to go to bat against my mother for me. Words cannot express how much it means to have somebody on my side for once. It's hard to wrap my head around it, really. My entire life has felt like it was me against the world, like a constant battle to prove that I'm not the person I've been labelled as. Twenty-three years of fending for myself and desperately seeking the approval of the one woman I loved more than anything in this world, even though she didn't love me back. And now I have not one, but two women in my corner. I don't know what I did to deserve this, but I thank my lucky stars that someone up there decided to cut me a break.

We pull up to the once quaint villa I used to call home. I'd tried to keep up with the maintenance on the place, but I'm no master builder. White paint is flaking off the weathered boards surrounding the deck, and the lawns are overgrown, spilling over the path. Dirt-smeared windows barely allow a glimpse inside.

We wade through the weeds and tall grass to the front door. Pulling it open, I take a deep breath and call out. "Mum? You home?" I know she is; her car is in the drive, and these days she rarely ventures far. If it wasn't for her disowning me, I would have considered it a privilege that she'd come to see me at the hospital when she did.

"What do you want?" Her words are spat like venom as she steps out of the kitchen and into the hall.

"I wanted to talk to—"

"What the fuck is she doing here?" she points her cigarette towards Grace who is standing behind me.

"You're gonna bring your father's ex-whore into *my* home!" she demands.

I don't know what I'd expected, but it certainly wasn't this. I can't seem to get any words to come out of my mouth as I stare at her with my mouth agape.

"Hello, Rosemary." Grace steps out from behind me. "It's been a long time."

*"It's been a long time,"* she mimics. "You're not fucking welcome. Get out of my house!"

Turning to Grace, I stutter, "I-I'm s-sorry."

"Don't apologise for her. You've done nothing wrong, Nathan." Her words are softly spoken, but her eyes are like molten lava as she stares at my mother. "Rose—"

"Don't call me that," she interrupts with a harsh whisper and I swear I can see tears in her eyes. "Only Robert…" she trails off, blinking rapidly.

Grace's entire demeanour changes and she takes a cautious step down the hall. "I'm sorry, I know how much you loved him."

"Don't. Don't you talk about him."

Taking another step forward, she continues. "I know it's hard. I loved him too," she whispers. My mother's head jerks around to face her with a steely gaze, but Grace holds her hand up to stop her. "It was never a competition. I could see how much he loved you. The way he looked at you, was like no one else was in the room. I could never compete with that. It was always you."

Slow tears trickle down my mother's cheeks. "Thank you," she whispers. In all my life, I don't think I've ever heard her utter those words before. All at once, her face crumples and she buries her head in her hands. Grace steps forward, pulling the burning cigarette from her hand.

"Come and sit down." She leads her over to the kitchen table, helping her to sit. "Rosemary? I know it hurts, and I know you need someone to blame, but," she glances up at me, reaching for my hand, "you can't keep doing this to Nathan. You lost your husband that day, but you're not the only one who lost somebody. Nathan lost his father, and I suspect, that's when he lost you too."

Shaking her head, my mother sniffs. "I have always been here for my boys."

"Have you really? You might have been here in the physical sense of the word, but you haven't really *been here* for them."

She sits back, looking as though she has a bad taste in her mouth. "What is this? You don't know a damn thing about me and my boys. You think you can just march in here and accuse me of shit?"

"No one's accusing anyone, Mum."

Her eyes snap to mine. "You, hush. You brought her here."

"That's exactly what I'm talking about, Rosemary. *I* offered to come with him. It's time you stop hiding behind your pain, and see what you have right here in front of you."

"I don't need parenting lessons from a spinster."

"Well you sure as shit need someone to open your eyes." Grace slams her hand down on the table, making my mother jump. "Do you even know where Noah is right now? Or that he spends his days getting high while Nathan does everything he can to protect him? Do you know that the only reason he went to prison, was because he was trying to save Noah from having to?"

"That's not true."

"It is, goddamn it! Nathan has spent his life trying to get you to notice him, to throw him a crumb of your love, but you don't even know he's there. He's a good kid and he deserves to be treated better."

"Did you put her up to this?" Mum glances at me, her eyes narrowed to slits before she turns back to Grace.

"No, he didn't. Just look at him, would you? *Really* look at him."

I stand there like an idiot while they argue. I've never had anyone stick up for me before and quite frankly, I'm at a loss as to what to do.

"Look at him." She enunciates each word, speaking slowly.

"I can't."

"You can."

"No, I can't!" She slams her fist down on the table, pushing up to stand and sending her chair flying. "He looks just like him. I can't," she sobs. "It hurts too much."

My throat clenches, strangling the sob that wants to burst forth from her words. "Mum?" It's barely more than a hoarse whisper, the words catching in my throat.

"I just… I can't." Her shoulders slump down and she turns away, walking to the kitchen counter. Bracing her hands against the edge, she leans forward as she weeps.

I don't know what to do. I'm torn between wrapping my arms around her and running. I've never seen her show so much emotion before.

"You're right. He does look like him. But that's a good thing." Grace stands up, walking over to her. She touches a hand to the small of her back, rubbing circles soothingly. "Instead of looking at him and seeing the hurt, try seeing the joy he brought you. You were the happiest couple I'd ever seen. He *loved* you with all his heart, and I know he wouldn't want you to be living this way. He did what he did because he needed to protect the precious gift you two made together. Don't let his death be for nothing. He would want you to be happy. He would want you to be a family."

She gestures for me to come join them. Tentatively, I reach out, my hand clamping down on her shoulder. When she lifts her eyes to mine, I see a tiny glimmer of light that I haven't seen for a long time. Something I thought I'd imagined.

She turns around and flings her arms around me, her hands clenching my shirt over and over, as if she can't quite hold enough of me. Together we stand, wrapped in each other's arms, weeping for the man we both lost.

# Chapter Thirty-two

Jess

"Hey, there she is." The hairs on the back of my neck stand on end, sending a shiver down my spine.

"Noah? Um, what are you… I thought you were…" The words jumble about in my brain as I try to speak. "You're out?"

He holds his arms out to the side, bobbing his head up and down. "Looks like it, doesn't it?"

"You, um… How are you feeling?" I ask cautiously, my grip on the stroller's handle tightening. Out for our daily walk, James and I had almost made it home when Noah popped up out of nowhere.

"Me? Oh, I'm just fine and dandy." He takes hold of the stroller, nudging me sideways, and begins walking alongside me.

"W-what are you doing?" My heart pounds in my chest, my eyes glued to James.

"Just walking with a friend. Isn't that what we are, Jess? I mean, you're practically my sister-in-law, from what I hear on the streets."

The penny drops. This is it. This is what Nathan was trying to protect me from. Noah, in his twisted way of thinking, is out for revenge.

I force out a laugh, but it sounds strained even to my own ears. "I don't know who you've been talking to, but they've got it wrong."

"Oh? So, my baby brother didn't just set you up in a house?" He raises one eyebrow at me, a sneer plastered on his lips.

*Shit. Think of something. Anything!*

I shake my head. "Nope. I mean, he did, but then we had a bust up. We're not... we're not together anymore." My voice shakes as I utter the words that have been haunting me the last few days. I haven't heard from him, and I have no idea if what I've said has any truth to it.

"Aww, now isn't that sad? The two lovebirds had a falling out. No more happy families," he taunts, his tone no longer friendly, and I wonder if he's on something. "You know what?" He looks at me with a grin before his eyes turn dark. "I don't believe you."

His eyes flick up and he nods. Those damn hairs on the back of my neck stick up again as I feel somebody come up behind me. Before I can turn around, a sharp pain burns the back of my head, and everything fades into blackness.

*Running so hard, but getting nowhere. My arms are pumping at my sides, sweat pours down my face and I can hear James wailing in the distance. Where the hell is he? I must find him! I try to force my legs to move faster, but it's like I'm running through quicksand.*

*"Here, take my hand!"* I look up to see Nathan, and his eyes reassure me that everything will be okay. I take hold of his hand, and he gives a hard yank, nearly ripping my arm from its socket. When I look up again, his face distorts into the sneer of his brother, Noah.

"No!" I scream, gasping for breath. Everything comes crashing back to me. "James!" *Where is he? Where am I? What the hell is going on?* "James!" His wails carry through from another room, and I go to move, but can't. I'm surrounded in darkness, with my wrists and ankles bound together behind my back. "Somebody help me!"

Footsteps thump closer and a sliver of light is cast over me as the door to my right opens. I blink against the brightness, trying to focus on who is there. I wiggle into somewhat of a sitting position.

"Hello? Can you help me? Please?"

"Can you help me?" Noah mimics in a high-pitched, sing-songy voice.

"Noah, please. Where's James?"

"Don't you worry, James is being taken care of." His tone doesn't give me much confidence.

"Please don't hurt him," I whisper. "I'll do whatever you want, just please... leave him alone."

He steps into the room, wielding a knife. He twists and turns it between his hands, the light from outside glinting off the edges, and panic begins to build. *Why can't I hear him anymore?*

"Please, Noah. Let me see him. Let me see that he's okay, and I'll do anything."

"Aww, isn't that sweet? I'm glad to hear that you're so willing to help me."

"Please, let me see him."

His face twists into a grimace as he snarls, "You don't get to make demands. You're the one tied up, in case you don't remember."

"You don't have to do this. Just tell me what you want, and I'll do it," I plead.

His hand rears back and stings my cheek. "For a smart girl, you don't listen very much, do you?"

*Keep him talking. You need to get out of this. Think.*

"Why are you doing this?"

He throws his head back, forcing out a laugh. "Oh, she wants to know why!" He drops his head, his eyes boring into mine. "Take a guess." Now that my eyes have adjusted to the light, I notice the way his body sways as if he can't quite keep still, his left eye twitches and they both have a glassy look to them, confirming my earlier suspicions that he's on something. Something that's fuelling his anger.

A sudden burst of defiance hits me and I lift my chin, staring him straight in the eyes. "You want me to guess? Okay. I guess that you don't have the balls to give up whatever it is you're injecting or snorting to take away the pain of your pathetic life, that you have to blame Nathan for making you face the truth." His eyes widen and he jerks his head backwards as if trying to get away from my words. It only spurs me on. "I think that you're too scared to do anything else, so you just waste your life away getting high while Nathan covers for you. You're just a sad little boy who can't take responsibility for his own actions."

"Shut up!" he screams, saliva coating his lips. "You don't know me!"

"I know enough!" I cry, angry tears spilling over my lashes. "Nathan was trying to help you! Open your eyes!"

When he rears his hand back again, I'm ready for it, bracing myself. "You shut your mouth, or I'll shut it for you," he seethes.

"I'll stop talking, as soon as you bring me my son."

"Well guess what?" He leans in, his face only an inch away from mine. "You remember my friend, don't you? The one who knocked you out? Well, he happens to be very good at snuffing out annoying sounds." He pushes his tongue to the front of his mouth, running it along his teeth. "Your boy, James? He's already gone."

# Chapter Thirty-three

Nathan

For the first time in as long as I can remember, I sit, holding Mum's hand on the couch. Grace left us an hour ago, and since then we've just been sitting here, getting to know each other again. I have to keep pinching myself to check that I'm not dreaming. It's the most surreal feeling.

"I'm so sorry, Nathan."

"Mum, stop. You don't have to keep apologising."

"Yes I do. I don't deserve your forgiveness." Her eyes well up again and she dabs a tissue under them.

I pat her hand. "It's okay."

"No, it's not." She lifts her eyes to mine and I can see the pain inside. "Every time I looked at you, it was a reminder of the man I lost. That piece of my heart I could never get back. My heart ached every time, so I just… stopped looking. I just left you to fend for yourself."

"Mum, I'm fine. Really. I have a job, and a girl I'm crazy about. It's Noah I'm worried about."

A flash of guilt shows on her face as she turns away. "That's another thing I screwed up. I knew what he was doing." She shakes her head. "I did. I heard people talking. It was just easier to turn a blind eye and pretend it wasn't real."

"I didn't exactly help the situation. I should never have covered for him. Maybe it wouldn't have gotten so bad."

She pins me with her gaze. "This is *not* your fault. If anything, it's mine. What kind of mother looks the other way when her son starts using?"

"The kind that's struggling with her own pain."

She smiles. "You always were the sweet one. Still. It's no excuse. Pain or no pain, I let you both down."

"It's never too late to change things," I say softly.

"I hope you're right." We sit in silence until the ping of my phone draws my attention. "You get that, I'm going to go and make a coffee. You want one?"

"Sure, sounds great." I reach for my phone, but notice Mum is standing in the doorway, staring at me. "What?"

"I just realised, I don't know how you have it," she says sheepishly.

"Milk and one please." I smile at the simplicity of it all. My mother is making me a cup of coffee.

"Got it," she says, heading down the hall.

My happiness is short-lived though.

**Noah has Jess.**

*What the fuck!*

My fingers quickly dial Darren's number and he picks up on the first ring.

"Nathan," he whispers.

"Talk to me, where is she?" I jump to my feet, pacing the floor.

"At that place you rented. I saw them carry her in there. She didn't look good."

"Fuck!"

"Nathan?"

"Yeah?"

"They had the baby too."

*They had the baby too.* Those words keep ringing in my ears, repeatedly. *They had the baby too.* If they did anything to hurt him, or Jess, I'd fucking kill them.

"You don't think he'll actually do anything to hurt them, do you?" Mum asks. After giving a brief explanation, she'd offered to help, driving me to where Darren was holed up.

"Are you forgetting what he did to me? If he's high, there's no telling what he'll do." My fist pounds the dashboard. "I should've been with her! I'll never forgive myself if anything happens to her."

"Calm down. We'll figure this out. He's taken her for a reason, and that's to get to you. So, if you want her to be safe, you need to face him with a level head. You're smart, Nathan. Use this." She taps her fingers on her temple.

"You're right, I'm sorry. It's just… she means everything to me. Her *and* James."

"I know. We'll get them back."

She pulls up down the road from Darren's hiding spot. With my hand on the door handle, I turn to her. "You've got your phone?"

"It's right here." She pats her pocket. "Be safe. Don't do anything stupid."

"I won't. Lock the doors, and lay your seat back, so you're not seen."

She nods and I climb out of the car. Hunching over, I scamper down the road to Darren's grandmother's place. Jumping the fence, I scan the area.

"Over here," he calls out in a loud whisper and I see him huddled in amongst the bushes. Running over to him, I peek through the fence at the house across the road. "I was just leaving Gran's when I saw him and some other goon carrying her inside. She didn't look as though she was awake, her legs were dragging behind her."

My chest tightens as I hear the blow-by-blow account. *I could've stopped this.*

"They've pulled all the curtains, so I don't know where they're keeping her, but I've kept an eye on it, and no one has come or gone. All I've heard is the baby crying, but even that stopped a little while ago."

I clench my eyes shut, slipping my thumb and finger under my glasses to pinch the bridge of my nose. *How could I let this happen? What the fuck am I going to do? Think, damn it!*

"What do you wanna do?"

I peer through the branches again. "Did anyone else see? You think the cops have been called?" I ask.

"Nah, don't think so. They had her arms slung over their shoulders, ya know, 'Weekend at Bernie's' style. I only noticed 'cause the kid was going nuts."

"Fuck!" I hiss. "If they so much as touch a hair on his head…"

"Hey, it's Noah. You don't really think he'd hurt a baby, do you?"

I turn my gaze onto him. "Don't I? After last time, I don't know what to expect with him anymore."

"Shit." He slaps a hand to my chest. "Look," he whispers, pointing across the road. A guy in black skinny jeans, black singlet and Doc Martens steps outside, a cigarette in his hand and a phone to his ear.

"Looks like now's our chance." Without taking my eyes off the son-of-a-bitch who's helping my brother, I quickly spout off a plan. "If what you saw is correct, then Noah is in there by himself. I need you to get this guy outta my way. Distract him somehow. I'll slip in through the back."

"No problem." Darren scurries to the far side of the property, keeping his body tucked low. When he reaches the edge, he slips around and jogs across the road. Hunching down beside the car out front, he jimmies the door open a fraction and wedges himself in the small gap. Seconds later, the car comes to life, rolling slowly down the road, the stereo blaring. Darren bolts down the road in the opposite direction. Geez that guy can run.

Meanwhile, Doc Martens is torn between taking chase after the car or Darren. He opts for the car as it begins to pick up pace, heading straight for another car parked up the road.

With him out of the way, I race across the road and around to the back of the house. All the curtains are closed, and the windows locked. Lucky for me, Noah and his goon aren't too smart. They obviously busted down the back door to get in in the first place, and it's barely hanging on the hinges.

Knowing it's only a matter of time before Doc Martens is back, I quickly take hold of the door, easing it open just enough for me to slip inside. It takes a minute for my eyes to adjust to the darkness, but when they do, I find myself face-to-face with the very man I was trying to avoid. Doc Martens.

# Chapter Thirty-four

Jess

My whole body turns numb and a high-pitched squeal
bounds around in my ears. I slump to the mattress on
the floor, the will to fight, gone.

*James.*

I want to scream, but when I open my mouth, no
sound comes out. I squeeze my eyes closed, hoping that
this is some kind of a nightmare, and if I squeeze hard
enough, I'll wake up and find James fast asleep in his
crib. I squeeze so hard that tears force their way out,
forming trails down my cheeks, and a puddle beneath
where I rest.

*James.*

He can't be gone. He can't be.

A whoosh of air hits my face and the stench of stale
cigarette smoke and sweat rushes over me.

"What's the matter, Jess? Cat got your tongue?"
Noah squats in front of me, his elbows resting on his
knees. "Not so brave now, are ya?" he taunts. "You're
gonna be a good girl now, and help me out. Or you'll
be next."

I drag my eyes open and stare right through him, tears clouding my vision. "Why would I help you?" I spit the words from my mouth.

He grips my chin in his hand, leaning in so close I can feel his breath on my face. "Because if you don't—" A crash down the hall stops him mid-sentence. "Fuck!" he screams, tossing my head back down to the mattress before rising to his feet. He stomps over to the door. "What the fuck—"

"Hello, Noah."

*Nathan.* I would recognise that voice anywhere. He came for me. *Just like the knight in shining armour.*

"Well, well, well. Look what the cat dragged in. Guess you're off the hook, for now, Jess." He turns and pins me with a dirty smirk.

"Let her go. This is between you and me."

"Tut, tut, little brother. No speaking out of turn, or I might just have to do something you'll regret." He slowly steps backwards, and I shrink as far back against the wall as possible.

"I said leave her alone."

"And I said shut it or I'll fucking hurt her!" Noah screams and in the distance, I hear the cries of a baby. My baby.

"James," I whisper.

Without taking his eyes from Noah, Nathan nods. "He's okay, Jess. I made sure of it." Relief washes over me at his words.

Noah lifts his palm to his mouth. "Oops, guess you caught me out. You didn't honestly think I could hurt a baby, did you?" All I can do is stare incredulously at him. "You on the other hand…"

"You wouldn't hurt her."

"Wouldn't I?" He snaps his head back around to face Nathan, brandishing the blade once more, twisting and turning it between his hands. "You don't know what I'm capable of, little brother."

"This isn't you. It's that shit you're on, it's making you do things, say things that you don't mean."

"That's where you're wrong, little brother. It makes everything feel goooood." He draws out the last word. "You should try it. You never know, you might like it." He swivels round to look at me, grinning. "I bet *you'd* like it."

"No… please… I don't want to," I whisper, watching him pat down his pockets until he produces a small plastic baggy filled with white powder. He rubs it between his thumb and finger, holding it up for us to see.

"Go on, Jess. Just a taste." He opens the bag, licks his finger and shoves it inside, before holding it out to me. "Go on, try it."

"N-no thanks."

"*N-no thanks,*" he mimics. His face takes on a menacing look and his eyes narrow. "I didn't ask. I'm telling you. Try it."

"P-please don't m-make me do this." I try to push even further into the wall, but there's nowhere else to go.

"You're going to refuse my kind gesture?" He cocks his head to the side and I catch a glimpse of Nathan edging closer.

"You d-don't want to w-waste it on me."

With one eyebrow raised, he stares at me a beat before nodding. "You're right. More for me!" he sings, rubbing his finger along his gums.

An almighty roar emits from Nathan as he lunges from behind. Noah fumbles, dropping both his blade and the baggy, powder spilling across the floor.

"Nooooooo!" he screams, diving to the ground to scoop up what he can. "That shit's expensive, you fuckwit!"

Nathan grabs the knife from where it landed, and tucks it into his back pocket before rushing over to me. "Are you okay? Did he hurt you?" His eyes rake over me from top to bottom, landing on my bruised cheeks.

"I'm okay. Just get me out of here, please."

"Anything for you." He scoops me into his arms and walks past Noah who is oblivious to us. "You need help, Noah. That's all I was ever trying to do for you."

When he snaps his head in our direction, his nose dusted in powder, his eyes are glazed and unseeing. "What are you talking about? Why are you here? Leave me alone!"

"Damn it, Noah!" Nathan growls, his green eyes glistening as he storms out the door.

# Chapter Thirty-five

Nathan

With Jess securely wrapped in my arms, I carry her over the lump that is Doc Martens, and through to the back room where I last saw little James. The minute her eyes land on his stroller, she whimpers and tears well up in her eyes.

"Nathan... I need to see him," she whispers. "Can you help me?"

I set her down on the floor and begin to untie the bindings holding her hostage. As soon as the last rope drops to the floor, she is on her feet, reaching into the stroller to take James in her arms. Cradling him against her body, she inhales his scent, all the while murmuring softly to him. "Shh, you're okay now, Mummy's got you."

It hits me how close I came to losing them today. I've never seen Noah like that before, not even when he attacked me. The effects seem to be getting worse every time I see him, and there's no telling what he could do. I can't risk anything else happening to Jess.

Placing a gentle hand on her shoulder, I say, "We need to leave. The amount he just snorted back there?" I point back to where we'd come from, "I don't know what that will do to him, but I don't think we should stay and find out. I couldn't bear it if... if..." I rake my hand through my hair, gripping the back of my neck.

"Okay." She nods and carefully places James back into the stroller, strapping him in. "Ready." Together, we carry the stroller over Doc Martens, and out into the darkening night.

I lead her across the road to where Darren is keeping watch. He jumps up from the bush when he sees it's us. "Shit, man, you got her!" he cries, flinging his hands in the air. "What the hell happened in there? Did you knock some sense into him?"

"Walk and talk," I say, heading down the road towards Mum's car. He quickly jumps in line. "We need to call the cops."

Stopping in his tracks, Darren grabs hold of my arm. "You're not serious."

"I am. He needs help."

Darren lowers his voice, looking side-to-side. "Man, you know I can't do that. I'm no snitch."

"You're not snitching. I am." I look back to the house I'd picked for Jess. "You didn't see him back there. He was crazy. And it's only going to get worse." I turn back to face him. "He was on the gear again. A lot of it."

"Shit."

"Yeah, I know. He's my brother though, ya know? I've got to help him. I should've done it a long time ago."

Grabbing my phone from my pocket, I make the call to Officer Delaney.

We walk on in silence for a few minutes before Jess puts her hand on my arm. "You did the right thing."

"Thanks. It doesn't feel like the right thing though."

"You said it yourself. He needs help. Anyone who cares about him will see that." She stops and looks around. "Where are we going?"

"See that car up there?" I point to the white Honda parked two houses up. "That's my mum."

"She's here?" Her brow crinkles with shock.

"Um… yeah. Before all this," I wave my hand between us all, "we got to talking. I think things might actually be different now."

"Oh, Nathan, that's great. I'm so happy for you." A smile lights up her face and I can't help but be amazed at how resilient she is.

"How do you do that?"

"What?"

I point at her face. "That. You're smiling, after what my brother just put you through."

She shrugs. "Sometimes you have to smile so that you don't cry. I know it wasn't the real Noah I was dealing with. I know he needs help. I'm just glad that you got there when you did."

"You're something else, you know that?"

"A good something?"

"The best." Her smile is so mesmerising, I can't take my eyes off her. "I'm so sorry for what he did. For making you think that he'd… that James was…" I can't even get the words out.

"It's not your fault, Nathan." She peers up at me, the soft caress of her fingers on my cheek. "Stop apologising for him," she whispers, resting her head against my chest. My arms fold around her, drawing her near. Knowing she's safe, and in my arms again is the best feeling in the world. I was a fool to walk away from her.

"I never should have left you on your own."

She pulls back, craning her neck to meet my eyes. "I can handle myself. I was just about to kick his ass. You just got in there before I had a chance." She grins, poking her tongue out between her teeth in jest.

"Oh of course, you're a right little Jackie Chan, aren't you?"

"Oh yeah, I got skills." She waggles her eyebrows at me and all I can do is laugh. This girl. God, I love her.

*I love her.* The realisation hits me square in the face. I am one hundred percent in love with this girl. I would do anything to hear her laugh, make her smile and keep her safe.

"Jess?"

"Mm?"

"I…" Darren grins goofily at me and I'm reminded that we're not alone. "Give us a minute?"

"Right, I'll just go and... ooh look, that's an interesting stone over there." He gives me the thumbs up and walks out of earshot.

"You were saying?" She looks up at me with humour in her eyes. I am amazed that this is the same woman who was tied up only minutes ago.

I take her hands in mine, noticing how perfectly they fit together. "When I took the job at the library, I never imagined I would meet someone like you. I don't know what I did to deserve you, and I don't care. I'm not giving you up again. I love you, Jess."

With fresh tears in her eyes, and a big grin on her face, she reaches up to cup my face in her hands. "I love you too, Nathan."

# Chapter Thirty-six

## Six months later

Jess

Bending over his crib, I plant yet another kiss on James' head before tip-toeing out the door. I pad down the hallway and out to the lounge, flopping down on the couch with a sigh. Motherhood, though rewarding, is exhausting. I don't remember the last time I slept through the night or had a clean pair of clothes on at the end of the day. Still, I wouldn't change it for the world.

James has made me a better person. I've done a lot of growing up over the last few months and with the help of some counselling, I found it in myself to forgive not only *him,* but Noah too. When Officer Delaney picked him up, he'd been barely coherent. They'd given him a longer stint in rehab, only this time he was under strict supervision. Once he was released, he was alright for a while, but it wasn't long before he relapsed again.

It took some work to get over it all, but in the end, it really came down to me wanting to be happy. I didn't realise how much time and energy I had wasted on being angry with them both.

"No sleeping," Nathan whispers in my ear, making me smile.

"I was just resting my eyes," I say, peeling them open one at a time. He lifts my feet and places them on his lap, gently massaging the aches away. "Mmmmm." My eyes flutter closed again as I lean my head back and relax.

"Rough day?"

"No more than usual. You?"

"Steady. I have some news."

"Mmm?"

"They want me to take some courses, become an actual librarian." He gives me that sexy lop-sided grin of his.

"Yeah? That's great! I'm really proud of you, babe."

"Thanks. I thought maybe we could celebrate with a drink. It's nothing fancy or anything, just a bottle of wine from the supermarket…"

I can't help but giggle at the cuteness of him. "Nathan, you know I don't need anything fancy. You and James are all I need." I stretch across to kiss him. "I'm also a cheap drunk, so supermarket wine is kinda my thing." I wink suggestively.

"Great! I knew there was a reason I liked you." He jumps up before I have a chance to slap his arm for that comment. When he returns from the kitchen, he has a strange look on his face, almost nervous. He hands me my glass, placing the bottle on the coffee table. He kneels on the floor and we clink our glasses together. "To our future," he says, tipping his back. I repeat his words and follow suit. "Another?" he asks, reaching for the bottle.

"Sure." I watch him out of the corner of my eye. "Is everything okay?"

He sweeps his hair to the side and adjusts his glasses before refilling our drinks. When he turns to hand me mine, he has the biggest grin on his face. "I've never been happier, Jess."

I can't help the smile that forms at his words. When he reaches into his pocket and pulls out a ring, I just about faint.

"The last six months have been the best six months of my life. I have never known a more selfless, strong and capable person than you. You've shown me what it is to truly love unconditionally, and I'm honoured that you've allowed me to be a part of you and James' lives. I can't imagine a life without you and I don't want to either." He pauses, reaching for my hand. "Jess, will you marry me?"

With tears streaming down my face, I nod, while he slides the ring on my finger. I hold my hand out, admiring the simple, yet beautiful piece of jewellery. "I love you," I whisper, pulling him in to me.

"Not as much as I love you," he says against my lips, sealing the deal.

# A note from the Author

Thank you so much for taking the time to read my novella, Never Judge a Book. These characters are close to my heart, and I hope you enjoyed getting to know them as much as I enjoyed creating them.

Please feel free to leave a review with your preferred retailer. Reviews help our words to be seen.

If you'd like to keep up to date with my new releases, you can sign up to my newsletter. I promise I won't spam you!


Thanks!

*Stacey*

# *Acknowledgements*

First of all, I need to thank my son for being the reason I needed to step up and make a change. You mean more to me than you will ever know.

To my husband, for always offering words of support, and allowing me the freedom to pursue this amazing career. I love you, babe.

To my amazing friend and proof-reader, Trina, for making sure I don't make an ass of myself and checking that I've crossed all the T's and dotted the I's.

To Shannon, for encouraging me and being a shoulder to cry on when I'm having a rough day, or someone to laugh with when we are celebrating our small victories in this crazy world of indie publishing. You make this a hell of a lot easier!

To Sloane, for giving me the motivation I needed and inviting me into the world of wordsprinting! It certainly helped me get my A into G to get this book done. All you wordcount sprinters are amazing and I hope to be able to one day keep up with you all!

To the seriously awesome group of friends in our reader group, the Ink Slinging Sisters, you guys rock! We must've done something right to have you all behind us!

To all the bloggers who work tirelessly, sharing the books that we (Indies) write and helping to spread the word of our genius. My hat goes off to you all.

And of course, to the readers, without whom, this would not be possible. I thank you for choosing my book out of the millions out there, and for going on this journey with me.

# Other Books by Stacey Broadbent

**Hollywood novel**
*Emma*

**Standalone**
*Never Judge a Book*
*Deep Heat*
*Fever*

**A Step in Time series**
*Dancing through the Storm*
*Dancing in Circles*
*Dancing with Destiny*
*A Step in Time: the complete series*

**Super Mum series**
*Frazzled*
*Frazzled and Frumpy*
*Frazzled, Frumpy and Fabulous!*
*Super Mum: the complete series*

**Dark sins novellas**
*Sins of the Flesh*
*Mine*

**Short Stories and Poetry**
*Musings, Mournings, and Misadventures*
*Musings, Mayhem, and Mystery*

**Anthologies**
*Scars to your Beautiful*
*Witching Hour: Vices and Virtues*

*The White Ribbon Collection*
*Key to my Heart*
*A Touch of Inspiration*
*No Place Like Home*
*Serendipity*

# Connect With Me

http://www.staceybroadbent.weebly.com

https://www.facebook.com/StaceyBroadbentAuthor

Broadbent's Bookish Babes: https://goo.gl/FY9wQN

https://www.amazon.com/author/staceybroadbent

Goodreads: https://goo.gl/YJ6dXa

https://www.instagram.com/authorstaceybroadbent/

https://www.bookbub.com/authors/stacey-broadbent

https://vm.tiktok.com/ZSJBb5bhL/

Newsletter sign-up: http://eepurl.com/cULu_f

# *About the Author*

Stacey resides in Ashburton, New Zealand with her husband and three children. She is a qualified proofreader, author, wife, mother, and self-proclaimed culinary goddess. When she's not busy writing or editing books, she enjoys reading and procrastinating on TikTok.

She absolutely loves hearing from readers, so please feel free to reach out via email, Instagram, or join her reader group, Broadbent's Bookish Babes. You can also sign up to her newsletter for up-to-date info on releases.

**www.staceybroadbent.weebly.com**